To the doctors in Catalunya: Montse Figuerola, Francesc Xavier Planellas, Pere Sola, Montserrat Verdaguer, who saved my life in 2006.

Chapter 1

It is one of the more surprising facts about Old England that one can still find families living in the same houses their ancestors built centuries before and on land that has belonged to them since before the Norman Conquest. The Gropes of Grope Hall are one such family.

Neither rich nor titled and having never excited the envy of their more powerful and influential neighbours, the Gropes had kept their heads down, worked fields still bearing the same names as they had in the twelfth century, and had gone about their business without taking the slightest interest in politics, religion or anything else that could have got them into trouble. In most cases this was not due to any deliberate policy. On the contrary, it had to do with inertia and the determination not to be burdened with ambitious and able offspring.

The Gropes of Grope Hall can be found in the County of Northumberland. They are said to be able to trace their ancestry back to a Danish Viking, one Awgard the Pale, who had been so seasick on the voyage over the North Sea that he had deserted the raiding party while it was sacking the nunnery at Elnmouth. Instead of raping nuns, as he was supposed to do, he had thrown himself on the mercy of a skivvy he had come across in the bakehouse, who was trying to make up her mind whether or not she wanted to be raped. Not being in the least beautiful and having twice been turned down by Viking raiding parties, Ursula Grope was delighted to be chosen by the handsome Awgard and led him away from the appalling orgy in the sacked nunnery to the isolated valley of Mosedale and the sod hut in which she had been born. The return of the daughter he had hoped he had seen the last of – and in the company of the enormous Awgard the Pale – had so terrified her father, a simple swine-herd, that he hadn't waited to find out the Viking's real intentions but had taken to his heels and was last heard of near York selling hot chestnuts. Having saved Awgard from the horrors of the return journey to Denmark, Ursula insisted that he save her honour as an unraped nun and do his duty by her. It is thus that the House of Grope is said to have been created.

Awgard changed his name to Grope, and so alarmed were the few inhabitants of Mosedale by his size and awful melancholy that Ursula, now Mrs Grope, was in time able to take possession of their thousands of acres of uninhabited moorland and eventually to establish the Grope dynasty.

As the centuries passed, the family legend and the dark secret of their origins encouraged succeeding generations of Gropes to keep themselves to themselves. They need hardly have bothered. The strain of melancholy and aversion to travel that had so afflicted Awgard continued in the Grope blood.

But it was the Grope women whose influence was most profound. To be twice rejected by Vikings, not normally discriminating in their choice of victims, as unworthy of violation had clearly left a psychological scar on the Founding Mother. Having secured Awgard she was determined never to let him go. She was also determined to hang on to the thousands of acres that his gloomy aspect and dangerous reputation had secured. That the Viking was in fact a deserter and terrified of the sea made both tasks easy. Awgard was always at home and refused even to go to the market in Brithbury or to the annual pig-gelding fair and mud-wrestling on Wellwark Fell. It was left to his wife and their five daughters to drive hard bargains at the market and indulge in the dubious activities at the fair. Since the daughters took after their father in size and strength and had inherited his red hair while combining these assets with the unprepossessing looks and determination of their mother, the result of the said mud-wrestling matches was never in doubt. Here, as in all matters involving the Grope women, the female line prevailed. Indeed, whereas in every other family, the eldest son succeeded to the estate, with the Gropes it was the eldest daughter who took over the Grope acres.

This became such a firmly established tradition that it was widely rumoured that, on those infrequent occasions when the firstborn was a boy, the infant was strangled at birth. Whatever the truth, it was certain that over the years the Gropes produced an unusually large number of baby girls, though this may have been due less to male infanticide than to the fact that either by choice or the Grope women's overt masculinity, the men they married tended to be somewhat effeminate.

Following the tradition laid down by the Founding Mother, the bridegrooms were forced to change their names to Grope. All too frequently they were forced into these marriages themselves. No ordinarily virile man would willingly have proposed to a Miss Grope even in his cups, and it may well have been as a result of the Misses Gropes' insistence on challenging local bachelors to a bout of mud-wrestling at Wellwark Fair that the event lost its attraction and finally died out. Even the most stalwart wrestlers hesitated before accepting the challenge. Too many young men had emerged from the ordeal half choked with mud and unable to deny that in the contest they had proposed to their opponents. Besides, the Grope girls were too formidably united to brook any denials. On one dreadful occasion a fiancé who had the temerity to say, when he could get the mud out of his mouth, that he would rather die than go to the altar and become Mr Grope, was hurled into the mud pool and held under until his determination was fulfilled.

To make matters worse, those male Gropes who survived the exigencies of being born alive had their careers chosen for them. They went into the Church if they could read or, if they couldn't (the majority weren't given the opportunity to learn), were sent to sea and seldom seen again. No sane man would have returned to Grope Hall to follow in their fathers' footsteps herding sheep, serving in the kitchen and only being allowed to speak when they were spoken to by their wives and mothers-in-law.

There was no escape. Early on in the family history a few of the husbands had managed to reach the dry-stone wall that bounded the Grope estate, and even, in one case, to get across it. But the desolate nature of the landscape combined with the fatigue of having to satisfy their wives' voracious appetites in bed made them incapable of getting any further. They were led back to the Hall by infuriatingly friendly bloodhounds specially trained to track down errant husbands and, after a severe dressing-down, were sent to bed supperless.

Even in less savage times the Grope women continued to dominate their menfolk and saw to it that as far as possible the existence of the estate went unnoticed. Of course the Hall was far removed from the original sod hut to which Ursula had first brought Awgard the Pale. Generations of strong-minded women with effeminate husbands to urge them on with talk of silk arrases, plastered ceilings and Venetian green chairs, not to mention the privacy and convenience of indoor water closets over outdoor earth ones, could not have been expected to leave the house in anything approximating to its original state. All the same, change came slowly and piecemeal. Nothing was wasted and nothing too ostentatious was added, at least externally, to draw attention to the Hall. Even the turf from the sod hut was reused to pack the gap between the planked bedroom floors and the ceilings below to deaden the sound of conjugal activities above.

By the nineteenth century Grope Hall had assumed the aspect of a large and relatively comfortable Northumbrian farmhouse, its thick grey stone walls and small windows doing nothing to hint at the strange traditions that had gone into its making and which still persisted in the mentality of the Gropes themselves. True, it was impossible to find a man in the district who was prepared to come within striking distance of a Miss Grope and, while the custom of mud-wrestling and its awful consequences had died out centuries before, the memory of those terrible occasions still lingered on in the neighbourhood. In fact, in some ways it contributed to the prosperity the Gropes enjoyed. A Miss Grope had only to put in an appearance at Brithbury market to empty the sale ring of all faintly marriageable men and drive the price of livestock down if the lady was buying, or up if she was selling.

By the 1830s the problem of finding husbands in Northumberland had become so severe that it was only the invention of the railway that saved the family from having to think seriously about recruiting fathers for their children from the local madhouse, with all the deleterious effects it would have had for future generations. Not that being married to a lunatic was necessarily an insuperable problem. In the past, several husbands had turned out to be so infertile or incurably impotent that desperate measures had had to be taken, either the kidnapping of passing strangers or paying for the sexual services of improvident tradesmen with large families to support. More than one traveller through Mosedale had undergone the horrifying experience of being waylaid by a Mrs Grope dressed as a man and forced to commit what he took to be an unnatural act before being stupefied with gin and opium and left unconscious in a ditch miles from Grope Hall.

The coming of the railways changed all that. It was possible to travel all the way to Manchester or Liverpool and return with a fiancé, albeit one who did not know he was engaged to be married until he was confronted by the Rev. Grope and forced to say 'I do' in the little chapel behind Grope Hall. The fact that several such bridegrooms were already married and had wives and families was happily overlooked, for this proof of their fertility only made them more attractive. Not only that, they also had a ready-made and perfectly understandable motive for changing their names. And at the same time, the knowledge that they were liable to prosecution and long prison sentences for bigamy gave them an attachment to Grope Hall they might not otherwise have had.

But the most persistent problem was that of first-born males when girls were wanted or, worse still, Mrs Gropes who failed to produce female offspring at all. The Registration of Births & Deaths Act of 1835 made the old remedy of strangling or suffocating baby boys at birth a decidedly risky procedure. Not that the family had ever admitted having recourse to such a thing.

A dearth of female heirs was a particular problem for Mrs Rossetti Grope who was seemingly incapable of producing girls.

'It's not my fault,' she wailed when a seventh baby boy arrived. 'Blame Arthur.'

This excuse, later to be proved scientifically accurate, did nothing to satisfy her sisters. Beatrice was furious.

'You shouldn't have picked the brute in the first

place,' she snorted. 'Any fool can see he's disgustingly licentious and masculine. Don't we know anyone round here who has a spotless record for fathering only girls?'

'There's Bert Trubshot over in Gingham Coalville. Mrs Trubshot has had nine lovely girls and – ' started Sophie.

'Bert the night-soil man? I don't believe it. An uglier man I never did see what with his acne and . . . are you sure?' asked Fanny.

Sophie Grope was.

'I am not being bedded by Bert Trubshot!' screamed Rossetti hysterically. 'My Arthur may not be the perfect husband but at least he's clean. Bert Trubshot's absolutely filthy.'

Her sisters looked at her with angry eyes. No Grope had ever refused to do her duty before. Even during the Plague when other farms in the district had shut their doors against strangers, a barren and widowed Eliza Grope had bravely dragged a number of terrified men misguidedly looking for the safety afforded by the remoteness of Mosedale to her bed and had given them succour. Not that her efforts had been rewarded in the way she hoped. She had died of the plague herself. But her example had set a standard for all later generations of Gropes to follow.

'You will lie with Bert Trubshot whether you like it or not,' Beatrice told Rossetti darkly.

'But Arthur will be furious. He's a very jealous man.'

'And a hopeless husband. In any case he won't know anything about it.'

'But he's bound to find out,' Rossetti said. 'And he's very keen on his loving.'

'Then we'll just have to see he loses interest in that side of things,' said Beatrice.

Three months later, when Rossetti was sufficiently recovered and her baby boy had been consigned to the usual orphanage in Durham, Arthur Grope was given an excessively strong dose of sleeping draught in his soup and had just enough time to comment that it tasted better than the soup usually did before falling asleep over the boiled mutton and carrots. Later that night he had a most unfortunate encounter with a broken bottle of brandy from which he never fully recovered.

In the meantime, Sophie and Fanny set off in a curtained carriage for Gingham Coalville to fetch Bert Trubshot. They found him going about his noisome task at two o'clock in the morning and while Fanny approached him from the front – ostensibly to ask if they were on the right road to Alanwick – Sophie, armed with a loaded blackjack, rendered him unconscious with a judicious blow to the back of his skull. After that it was a simple matter to drive him back to Grope Hall where, after he had been scrubbed and blindfolded and liberally anointed with several bottles of perfume, given a great many oysters and some crushed pearl, he performed his duty in a state of hallucinatory delirium brought on by concussion.

Even Rossetti found the experience less distasteful than she had expected and felt a sense of loss when he was finally drugged and driven back to Gingham Coalville. What Bert Trubshot felt when he was found stinking of perfume and stark naked on the doorstep of the Trubshot cottage was the back of his wife's hand and a degree of regret that he had ever married such a violent and unlovely woman.

Arthur Grope was feeling even worse. Lying in Wexham Hospital he was painfully aware of what had happened to him but couldn't for the life of him imagine how or why it had happened.

'Isn't there something you can do?' he asked the doctors in an already altering voice, only to be told there wasn't much left to do anything with and anyway he shouldn't have drunk so much brandy. Arthur said he couldn't remember having drunk any brandy at all, not a drop, because he'd been a teetotaller all his life but that, if what the doctors told him was true and his only pleasure in life had gone for good, he was damned well going to drink like a fish in future.

Arthur's resolution to become a full-blown drunk was reinforced when, nine months later, Rossetti Grope gave birth to an unusually ugly daughter with black eyes and dark hair and none of the features that had distinguished the boys he had previously fathered. He died a deeply bitter and alcoholic castrato a year later and was followed to the grave shortly afterwards by Rossetti and her daughter, both of whom caught pneumonia during a singularly cold and wet winter.

Fortunately for the Grope family, Fanny made good the shortcomings of Rossetti, producing seven baby girls without benefit of clergy by making regular repeat visits late at night to Gingham Coalville where, being less sensitive and hygienic than her late sister, she enjoyed the attentions of Bert Trubshot. Thanks to a night-soil man, the female Grope line was once again secure.

Chapter 2

By the middle of the nineteenth century the gentrification of British society, which had begun almost a hundred years before in the South, finally reached Mosedale and Grope Hall. The Gropes, having already installed indoor water closets and Venetian green chairs, did their best to ignore this further assault on the grounds that like all previous fashions it would soon pass. But inevitably even Beatrice, now the dominant mistress of the Hall, finally succumbed to the lure of antimacassars and the cluttered furnishings that had been popular elsewhere fifty years before. The old tin baths that had sufficed the family for their annual ablutions for so many years were discarded and replaced with a huge iron bath equipped with taps and regular cold and occasional hot water and the female Gropes were to be found bathing at least once a week.

But for the husbands and the odd son still lurking about, things continued much as they had before. Grope menfolk brewed ale for their wives and distilled various lethal spirits which they called brandy or gin according to their colour as they had for generations, and if they were lucky, or if their wives desired their services that night, were allowed to take the occasional bath in a nearby river.

Gentrification aside, men and women generally went about their business as though nothing material would ever change. But they were wrong.

At the start of the twentieth century coal was found on the estate in larger quantities than ever before and in seams so thick and in such close proximity that not even Adelaide Grope, the one daughter to possess a shrewd business mind and acting head of the family in place of the now senile and bedridden Beatrice, could resist the prospect of immense wealth. The naval arms race with the Kaiser's Germany had just begun and the demand for coal to build and fuel dreadnoughts was enormous. A narrow railway line was built along the desolate valleys, trucks loaded to the brim trundled down to the great ironworks and shipyards sixty miles to the east and returned filled with sturdy men to work the mines.

Almost overnight the Gropes became relatively rich,

both in money and in an apparent surfeit of men who might service the Grope girls, even if they wouldn't marry them. But it wasn't to be. The sinister reputation of the family, and nine awful dogs, descendants of the friendly bloodhounds but now decidedly unfriendly, deterred any men, whether new to the district or not. So did the girls. In truth, Beatrice's daughters, all five of them, retained too many of the physical attributes of their forebears to hold any attraction for even the most desperate man. Soon the miners steered clear of Grope Hall altogether, moving only in groups, a single man being an easy target. From the windows of the Hall predatory eyes watched them clamber out of the empty coal wagons in the morning and cling to the sides of full ones returning at night. There was nothing the Grope girls could do.

Adelaide, however, who retained the ruthless attributes of her ancestors, still found ways to exploit both the new-found Grope riches and the sudden increase in available men. For one thing, she had foreseen the taxation problems that lay in the possession of ostentatious wealth. To ensure that the taxation authorities would be unable to establish the true profit from the mine she had drawn up the contract herself. It was an extraordinary document, to put it mildly. All profits were to be in gold sovereigns payable on a monthly basis, and to be brought to the Hall by the chief accountant of the mining company who was himself privately guaranteed 5 per cent of the unrecorded total.

Finally she had persuaded Beatrice, legally still head of the family, to sign the contract with the mining company in the presence of two terrified doctors, one a psychiatrist at a mental hospital, together with a notary public. Since Beatrice had been confused to the point of dementia at the time, Adelaide had paid extravagantly for this privilege, forking out a substantial sum by way of bribery to guarantee the doctors' and the notary public's acquiescence that Beatrice was in her right mind

Having secured the Grope family fortunes, Adelaide turned her attention to the vexing problem of securing the female line. And in the tradition of her forebears she concluded that kidnap and enforced captivity was the only viable solution.

Noting the inroads to the Grope estate afforded by the new railway lines, Adelaide embarked upon an ambitious plan by which to strengthen security and to ensure that any stray miners, once seized, stayed seized. After a particularly successful night-time sortie which saw two unsuspecting fellows contentedly fishing Mosedale River wake up several hours later trussed up like chickens under the watchful eye of two of the larger Grope daughters, these precautions took on a new urgency. A notice on the gate went up warning anyone attempting to get down to Grope Hall to 'BEWARE THE SPANISH FIGHTING BULLS' and indeed two lithe and dangerous bulls were loosely tethered next to the rough track that served as a drive to the house.

After a number of mishaps largely involving gored postmen and an entire absence of any letters, however urgent, for the Grope household, a box had been fastened to the wall beside the gate for the mail.

Adelaide had gone further to ensure that no one intruded and that, once in, no one would get out. The top of the wall had been implanted with iron spikes while especially thickened steel barbed wire was arranged on more iron stakes on the near side of the wall. In fact these precautions were almost counter-productive. The Gropes' reputation had for centuries sufficed to keep the public at bay and that they had erected what amounted to a formidable defence system aroused a great deal of curiosity. People came over from Brithbury and even further afield to look at the spikes and the peculiar black bulls and of course went home to spread the word that the Grope family's old traditions had evidently not died out.

'They must be trying to keep some poor devil trapped in the place' was the general opinion in the Moseley Arms. 'Must be a very fierce fellow too to need all those spikes and wire and all. Cost a small fortune to put that lot up at that. Them rich, them Gropes, to afford to do all that. Goodness only knows where they got them bulls from.'

'Spain supposedly. It says so on the noticeboard.'

An old man by the fire grinned. 'Supposedly is right,' he said. 'Bought the brutes in Barnard Castle is my opinion. No more fighting bulls than I am.'

'I wouldn't want to risk going down there for all that,' said another man. 'It's them nine dogs frighten the lights out me. More like wolves than blood-hounds they are.'

News of this gossip reached Adelaide. It didn't worry her. But the accumulation of so much more wealth than they had ever possessed before, and its effect on her sisters, did. The two unfortunate fishermen had lasted a mere season in the Grope household with only a phantom pregnancy to show for it. And the continued presence of so many brawny miners passing below the house every day unsettled both the Grope women and the tethered bulls. The former spent their time yearning for marriage. The latter yearned too, but for an unspecified kind of consummation.

After several years enduring this pent-up desire Adelaide finally allowed the younger Grope women to go out into the world with sufficient incomes to live in a style to which they were unaccustomed. She wisely kept the bulls tethered.

Freed from the seclusion of Grope Hall and the dominance of Adelaide, the newly released female Gropes rapidly found husbands and settled down in towns and farms across southern England with husbands who knew nothing of the Gropes' history. By the outbreak of the First World War, Adelaide herself had forced the chief accountant into marrying her by threatening to expose his acceptance of the percentage he received from cooking the books. And a year later she had given birth, much to her joy and to everyone else's amazement, to a baby girl. By then, mad old Aunt Beatrice had died and Adelaide, determined to celebrate, had completely transformed the interior of Grope Hall while the exterior remained as gaunt as ever. Inside, the rooms were no longer so far behind the times as they had been. Adelaide had had them redecorated and furnished in the most modern style since finding out from the chief accountant that she might write off the refurbishment as a business expense. Only the scrubbed wooden tables and benches in the kitchen and in what was called the study remained. It was here that business was conducted, and Adelaide had no intention of giving away any indication of her wealth. For safety's sake most of the gold she had converted her profits into was hidden in an unnecessarily deep grave and covered with earth under the stone-flagged floor of the ancient chapel unknown to anyone except Adelaide herself together with the Reverend Nicholas Grope who was never allowed off the premises so scarcely counted. In any case, the effort of digging the grave that contained the gold had damaged his back so badly and he was so old he spent most of his time in bed and was incapable of going anywhere even had he been allowed to.

The twentieth century eventually caught up with the family, though not in the way that might have been expected. The demands of industry during the

Great War exhausted the last of the coal in the mine which had already had to be evacuated twice because of flooding and roof falls. But in the end, the war did relatively little to affect the lifestyle of the Gropes.

The first catastrophe came with the Spanish influenza which carried off 20 million people across Europe – more than had died in the fearful War itself. By then Rev. Nicholas's successor had already died of heart failure and had, quite literally, taken the secret of the family treasure with him as the gold was reburied below his body by Adelaide's daughter. Finally the Spanish flu killed Adelaide, her daughter and her husband, the chief accountant, who in latter days had largely run the estate under his wife and imperious daughter's direction. Adelaide's successor as head of the Grope family was a widow, Mrs Eliza Grope, who had returned to the Hall on her husband's death, deeply grateful to General Ludendorff for having rid her of her husband, Major Grope in his offensive of March 1918.

On taking charge, Eliza soon restored the old Grope ways since the exhausted mine was no longer a source of income. She'd never enjoyed the modern lifestyle of the South with its stifling politeness, its social niceties and need to conform, and she'd particularly objected to her husband's assumption that he was the head of the household and she was merely a superior sort of servant. Determined to reassert her dominance, she chose as the new Reverend Grope the orphaned son of a Grope cousin who had been killed in a Zeppelin raid on London. His father, having remarried, no longer wanted the gormless adolescent around and was happy to have Eliza send him to a minor theological college.

Even after the Second World War, and long after Eliza had been succeeded by Myrtle Grope, yet another widow well rid of her partner by the battlefield, the family refused to entirely move with the times. Fields were still turned by horse-drawn ploughs, haystacks retained and cows milked by hand. The bloodhound numbers were reduced to six following an unfortunate incident with one of the bulls, but by and large, had Ursula Grope and Awgard the Pale returned from the twelfth century, they would have been proud to recognise Grope Hall as their own.

It was to this isolated estate and ancient farmhouse that, as the new millennium dawned, Belinda Grope, niece of the now aged Myrtle, brought a young and largely callow youth named Esmond Wiley.

Chapter 3

Esmond Wiley's boyhood had been a disturbed one. This was largely due to his name.

It was hardly his fault, or even that of his father, that his surname was Wiley, though in his darker moods Esmond had been known to wish that Mr Wiley had remained a bachelor. Or had he felt compelled to marry, which was self-evidently the case, that he had remained celibate or, and this was self-evidently not the case, that he had taken precautions not to impregnate his wife. Not that Esmond blamed his father. Mrs Wiley was not a woman to be denied her right to motherhood. A large and unfortunately cheerful woman, with an insatiable appetite for the most mawkish and deplorable romantic fiction, she had acquired an equally insatiable lust for love. Or to put it another way, she lived in a world in which men, gentlemen of course, proposed marriage passionately on clifftops under a full moon with the waves crashing on the rocks below and were accepted with a mixture of delight and modesty before crushing their maidenly fiancées to their manly breasts.

It has to be said that this was not exactly what Mr Wiley had done. He wasn't a very manly man in the first place, and being a bank manager in Croydon he had done his level best to resist the slight strain of passion that ran, or rather limped, in the Wiley family. All the same, Mrs Wiley, then Vera Ponson and aged twenty-eight, had persuaded him to propose to her. Worse still, she had insisted on going through the clifftop ritual she had read about so often, and the couple had driven down to Beachy Head when the moon was at its fullest, attired in evening dress which seemed the closest approximation to the satin bustiers and velvet pantaloons referred to so frequently in the romances the future Mrs Wiley favoured. Other things being equal the occasion, or tryst as Vera called it, might yet have fulfilled her wildest dreams. But other things weren't. The full moon was there somewhere but put in only fitful appearances, hidden for the most part by low clouds. Vera Ponson refused to be disappointed. To her way of thinking those clouds were scudding, and the wind on the clifftop gusted very authentically five hundred feet above a presumably troubled sea. It was too dark to see whether the sea really was troubled or not and in truth, even if it had been as bright as the full moon might have made it, Mr Wiley, by nature and occupation an exceedingly cautious man, had been disinclined to look. He also suffered from a height phobia. It was a measure of his love for Vera or, more accurately, his desperation to attain those home comforts that his married friends appeared to enjoy and which Vera's innocent romanticism seemed to promise, that he had allowed himself to go anywhere near the perpendicular cliff face in the first place. He had only remembered on the journey down there that it was Beachy Head from which so many people had hurled themselves to their deaths, and confronted with the ghastly reality of the sheer drop which he could see would be impossible to survive, his fear quadrupled.

It was this terror rather than any real passion that had impelled Mr Wiley to propose to Vera with amazing speed and then clasp her to his palpitating heart. He was helped as well by a sudden gust of wind which had practically swept him off his feet at that very moment. With his bride-to-be in his arms, and a very heavy bride-to-be to boot, he felt far safer and, as if to celebrate their union, the moon, as full and brilliant as Vera had wished, shone through a gap in the clouds and illuminated the couple.

'Oh my darling, how I have waited for this moment,' Vera murmured ecstatically.

But so it seemed had two policemen. Alerted by a passing motorist who had seen the car and had phoned the station to report that another pair of lunatics were evidently about to commit suicide, they had crept up on the lovers with the utmost stealth.

'Now now, it's going to be all right,' one of the policemen had said as their flashlights added a new brilliance to the scene.

It had not been all right. Horace Wiley had objected to having to identify himself as a bank manager presently residing at 143 Selhurst Road, Croydon, almost as much as the imputation that he had been about to take his own life or, as the sergeant had rather tactlessly put it, 'the easy way out'.

In later life, Horace Wiley was inclined to conclude that there had been a prophetic quality about the expression, but at the time he was more concerned with the possible consequences for his career prospects if it ever got out that, again in the words of the police sergeant, he 'made a habit of driving down to Beachy Head at full moon in fancy dress to propose to strange women', which was more or less what Vera had explained he had been doing. Mr Wiley wished she'd kept her trap shut, a preference which throughout their married life together proved as worthless as it was now, while Vera had found the suggestion that she was a strange woman so offensive that the sergeant came to regret it himself. And then it began to rain.

In short, from these inauspicious beginnings, the

marriage in St Agnes's Church chosen for its literary association (Vera had been deeply affected by the poem at school) and the honeymoon on Exmoor (thanks this time to Lorna Doone), a son and heir emerged and was named Esmond. And it was because of the name Esmond, rather than the more innocuous Wiley, that the offspring of Horace and Vera's union suffered such a tormented boyhood.

Esmond was called Esmond after a character in a particularly virulent love story his mother had been engrossed in shortly before his birth. In Vera's dazed and drug-addled state following a horribly difficult labour in which Horace Wiley had been of little and no use, his fear of blood being almost equal to his fear of heights, she found some comfort in picturing the fictional Esmond. A he-man in buckskin breeches with his shirt open to the waist, exposing an immensely virile chest and a mane of the blackest locks windswept on an open moor or, more often, standing on a rocky promontory above a wave-tossed sea, he seemed the best model for a boy who she determined should be nothing like his timorous and decidedly lacking-in-romance father.

Exposed so early to such awful literary influences, it was perhaps not surprising that Esmond Wiley took at an early age to an activity best described here as lurking. While other boys ran and shouted and skipped and larked about and generally behaved in a boy-like fashion, almost from the moment he first walked

Esmond only ever lurked about the place in a manner that was both sneaky and melancholic.

From Esmond's point of view, his behaviour was entirely understandable. It was bad enough to be called Esmond but to see also the image of Vera's romantic hero littering the house and on sale in every bookshop and newsagent he went into was enough to make even an insensitive boy aware that he could never live up to his mother's hopes and expectations.

And Esmond was not an insensitive boy. He was an acutely self-conscious one. No child with his legs and ears, the former thin and the latter thick and protruding, could fail to be aware of himself. Nor could he fail to be equally aware of the shortcomings of his mother who brought to child-rearing the same uncritical and sentimentally old-fashioned attitudes she brought to reading.

To say that she doted on Esmond, or even that he was the apple of her eye, would be to fall far short of the frightful adoration to which the poor boy was subjected. Whenever Vera spotted her son she was particularly addicted to announcing, in public and in a loud voice, 'Look at this divine creature. His name is Esmond. He is a love child, my sweet darling boy, a true love child,' a term she had picked up from *The Coming of Age of Esmond*, ostensibly by Rosemary Beadefield but actually composed by twelve different writers each of whom had written a chapter.

The fact that Vera had completely misunderstood

the expression, and was announcing to the world that her son had been born out of wedlock and was, as his father frequently thought though never dared say, a little bastard, never crossed her mind. It didn't cross Esmond's either. He was too busy enduring the jeers, catcalls and whistles of any and everyone who happened to be in the vicinity at the time.

To have a blowsy mother who takes one out shopping and announces to the world at large, even if that world at large is merely Croydon, that 'this is Esmond' is bad enough, but to be known as 'a love child' as well is to put iron into the soul and red-hot iron at that. Not that Esmond Wiley had a soul, or if he did, it wasn't a particularly noticeable one, but the gaggle of neurons, nerve endings, synapses and ganglia that constituted what little soul he might be supposed to have had were so churned up by these repeated and excruciating disclosures that there were times when Esmond wished he was dead. Or that his mother was. Indeed, a normal, healthy child might well, and justifiably, have done something to achieve one or other of these desirable ends. Unfortunately, Esmond Wiley was not a normal, healthy child. There was too much of his father's caution and timidity in him. Small wonder perhaps that he took to lurking, hoping to avoid notice and forced to endure another of his mother's public announcements.

Esmond's likeness to Horace Wiley was also a distinct handicap. Other fathers might have been delighted to have a son who so closely resembled them and whose characteristics were almost exact clones of their own. Mr Wiley's feelings were very different. Over the years of his marriage he had done his utmost to persuade himself that his sole motive for such a rash and disastrous matrimonial investment had been to ensure that the world would be spared the production of any more cautious and timid Wileys with spindly legs and protruding ears. Accordingly, this self-delusive argument went, he had chosen for his wife a tall woman with substantial legs and well-proportioned ears who would bear children (progeny, he called them) of such mixed ancestry that they would be approximately normal. In short, they would be standard products, a choice blend of bravado and timidity, brashness and self-effacement, vulgar sentimentality and cautious good taste who would lead rational and productive lives and wouldn't feel under any obligation to marry wholly unsuitable wives out of a sense of public duty and eugenics.

Esmond Wiley made a mockery of his father's hopes. He resembled Mr Wiley so precisely that there were moments in front of the shaving mirror when Horace had the terrifying illusion that his son was staring back at him. The same large ears, the same small eyes and thin lips, even the same nose, confronted him. Only Horace's legs were spared this awful symmetry being hidden in striped pyjamas. All else was revealed, grossly apparent.

And there was something even worse, though the shaving mirror did not show it. Esmond Wiley's cast of mind, as well as his appearance, was exactly that of his father. Timid, cautious, above all a sad and melancholic lurker and, like his father, possessing a complete aversion to his mother's taste in reading. In fact, Vera's attempts to get him to read the books she had been so influenced by, so infatuated by, in her adolescence physically sickened him, and on the few occasions when he couldn't be found lurking he was often discovered in the bathroom with his head strategically positioned above the bowl.

In short, there was not a sign of his mother's cheerful flamboyance, no manifestation of her good-hearted romanticism and not a hint of that passionate self-indulgence and vigour that had played havoc with Mr Wiley's sensibilities on their honeymoon. Whatever passions and self-indulgences Esmond possessed – and there were days when Mr Wiley doubted the boy had any – were so well hidden that Mr Wiley occasionally wondered if he was autistic.

At ten and even eleven years, Esmond was a singularly quiet child who communicated, when he spoke at all, only with Sackbut the cat, a neutered (a symbolic act on Mrs Wiley's part and one that had more to do with Horace Wiley's lack of performance than with Sackbut's personal propensities), obese animal who slept around the clock and only roused himself to eat.

Things might have gone on this way for ever, with

Esmond conversing only with the impotent Sackbut and lurking in Croydon corners and never going near Northumberland let alone any of the Gropes, had puberty not had a peculiar impact on the boy.

At the age of fourteen, Esmond suddenly changed, and in direct contrast to the timidity of his early years took to expressing his feelings with a vehemence that was deafening. In fact, quite literally deafening. The day before Esmond's fourteenth birthday, Mr Wiley, returning from an enervating day at the bank, was appalled to find the house reverberating to the sound of drums.

'What the hell's going on?' he demanded, with a great deal more force than usual.

'It's Esmond's birthday and Uncle Albert has given him a set of drums,' Mrs Wiley replied. 'I told him I thought Esmond might be artistic and Albert says in his opinion Esmond could be musically talented.'

'He said what?' Mr Wiley shouted, partly to express his incredulity and also to make himself heard above the din.

'Uncle Albert thinks Esmond is musical and just needs encouraging. He's given him a set of drums. I think it's very sweet of him, don't you?'

Mr Wiley kept his thoughts about Uncle Albert to himself. Whatever motives Vera's brother Albert might have had in distributing a set of large drums to an unquestionably highly disturbed adolescent – and from the infernal beat of the things they were very mixed indeed – 'sweet' was not the adjective Horace would have applied to Albert. Insane? Yes. Evil? Yes. Diabolical? Yes. But 'sweet'? A definite no.

Vera was devoted to her brother, and besides, Albert Ponson was a large and florid man who ran a distinctly dubious business involving supposedly second-hand cars which, in a surprising show of honesty, he advertised as 'pre-owned'. That the business was in Essex and that, as a sideline, he had a half-share in a pig farm with a DIY abattoir attached, hardly inclined Horace Wiley to object at all strongly to his brother-in-law's dreadful birthday present. He'd been up to Ponson Place, a sprawling bungalow set back from the road in ten acres of farmland, and the beastly man had insisted on showing him round that appalling slaughterhouse. As a result Horace had fainted at the sight of so much blood and eviscerated carcasses. When he recovered from this terrible visit, he'd come to a definite conclusion: too many of Albert Ponson's competitors in the used-car business had chosen to retire very hurriedly – or, in the case of one or two more obstinate dealers, to disappear altogether, ostensibly for Australia or South America – for comfort. The fact that Albert had found it advisable to turn his big bungalow into what amounted to a miniature fortress with bullet-proofed and mirror-glazed window glass and steel-lined doors throughout only added to Horace's fear of him. No, he couldn't even think of mentioning those damnable drums. The bloody man was a gangster. He was sure of that.

In an attempt to escape the reverberations coming from the drums, Horace found it expedient to go to the bank far earlier in the morning than usual and to return home a lot later at night. Vera began to believe that Horace was trying to avoid her and that it was the call of the pub rather than the call of work keeping him out late and indeed there was some truth to her suspicions. Be that as it may, it was left to the neighbours to complain about the savage din issuing – sometimes until two in the morning – from Esmond's bedroom. Mrs Wiley did her best to fight back but the arrival of the Noise Abatement Officer at the height of one of Esmond's most frenzied assaults on the drums, and the threat of prosecution if he continued, finally persuaded her to listen to reason.

'All the same, I want him to have music lessons, private lessons,' she told her husband, and was surprised to find he had already made enquiries and had found an excellent piano teacher who had the advantage of living in an isolated cottage ten miles away.

Esmond went there five times before being asked not to come again.

'But why not? There must be a reason, Mr Howgood,' Mrs Wiley said, but the music teacher only muttered something about his wife's nerves and Esmond's difficulty with scales.

Mrs Wiley repeated her question.

'Reason? A reason?' said the pianist, evidently finding the greatest difficulty in associating Esmond's awful idea of music with anything faintly rational. 'Apart from not having my piano beaten to death . . . well, that is the reason.'

'Beaten to death? What on earth do you mean?'

Mr Howgood contemplated the empty space on the mantelshelf where his wife's favourite Bernard Leach vase had stood until Esmond's violent thumping on the piano had reverberated it off into the fireplace.

'The piano is not entirely a percussion instrument,' he said finally in a taut voice. 'It is also stringed. And it is not a drum, Mrs Wiley, it is definitely not a drum. Unfortunately your son finds it impossible to make this distinction. If he has any musical gift . . . let's just say he should stick to drumming.'

Defeated in the matter of her son's musical development, Mrs Wiley still persisted in her belief that the newly transformed Esmond was naturally artistic. However, after he had expressed himself visually with an indelible felt-tip pen in the downstairs toilet, even she had some reservations about him becoming a painter. Mr Wiley's reservations were total.

'I am not having the house desecrated simply because you think he's Picasso come back from the grave, and the cost . . . when I think of the cost of redecoration! The repairs will come to several hundred pounds thanks to that damned felt-tip pen.'

'I'm sure Esmond didn't know it would permeate the plaster like that.'

But Mr Wiley wasn't to be diverted.

'Seven coats of emulsion and it still showed through, and where has he seen a woman's whatnot like that? That's what I'd like to know.'

Mrs Wiley preferred not to look at it like that.

'We don't know it was what . . . what you think,' she said, drawing him into a trap. 'That's just your dirty imagination. I didn't see it as any part of anyone's anatomy. I saw it as purely abstract, as line and shape and form and – '

'Line and shape and form of what?' demanded her husband. 'Well, I'll tell you what Mrs Lumsden saw it as. She – '

'I don't want to hear. I won't listen,' Mrs Wiley said, and then saw her opportunity. 'And how do you know what she saw? Are you saying Mrs Lumsden told you she thought it was a . . .'

'Mr Lumsden did,' said Mr Wiley as his wife ground to a halt before the unspeakable. 'He came in to the bank to ask about extending his overdraft and just happened to mention at the same time that his damned wife had been fascinated to see the drawing of a woman's fanny on our lavatory wall when she came round for coffee with you the other morning.'

'Oh no, she can't have. It had been painted over by then.'

'So it had. Twice but it still came through the

emulsion. Mrs Lumsden told her husband it actually grew as she sat there.'

'I don't believe it. How could it grow? Drawings don't grow. She's invented the whole thing.'

Horace Wiley said that was hardly the point. The point was that Mrs Lumsden had seen the . . . well, the bloody thing growing . . . all right, not growing, appearing through the emulsion as she sat there, and that scoundrel Lumsden had the nerve to try to increase his overdraft by threatening to let it be known that the Wileys, or more precisely Horace Wiley, made a habit of drawing vulvas, – yes, to hell with whatnots and fannies, let's get down to nitty-gritties – on the wall of his lavatory, and that being the case –

'You are not going to let him? You can't possibly allow him . . .' Mrs Wiley squawked.

Horace Wiley seemed to look at his wife for the first and, possibly, the last time.

'Of course I denied everything,' he said slowly, and paused. 'I told him to bloody well come and check for himself if he didn't believe me. Which is why the plasterers are arriving to repair the rest of the damage tomorrow.'

'More damage? What damage?'

'The damage done by a litre of Domestos, a hammer and a blowtorch I paid twenty-five pounds for. And if you don't believe me, go and have a look yourself.'

Mrs Wiley had already gone and from the silence that followed Horace knew that for the first time in their married life he had achieved the seemingly impossible. She had nothing to say and the question of Esmond's artistic education was shelved for good.

Mrs Wiley had other matters to occupy her mind now and the main one was how very manly she found her husband in this moment of assertiveness. Gazing at the vandalised cloakroom wall she couldn't help wondering whether Horace might be persuaded to try on the, to date largely unworn, buckskin breeches she had bought him as a wedding present. All in all it might turn out to be rather a good thing that the newly loud Esmond no longer lurked.

Chapter 4

Unfortunately for Vera, Horace's assertive moment was exactly that – a moment. He was back to his timorous ways in no time at all. And if in part it had been his mother's ambition which had caused Esmond to react with such apparently mindless violence against anything faintly artistic or even sensitive, then his father's influence over the next few years continued to be hardly less baleful.

Mr Wiley's profession no doubt contributed to his old-fashioned insistence that two plus two must invariably make four, that books had to balance and that money didn't grow on trees but had to be earned, saved and accrue interest, and that the second law of thermodynamics applied as much to human affairs as it did to the realm of physics. Or, as he put it to Esmond one sultry afternoon when, much against both their wills, father and son were sent for a 'nice' walk on Croham Hurst, 'Heat always flows from something that is hot to something that is cold, never the other way round. Is that clear?'

'You mean something that is cold like an ice cube can't warm a gas fire?' said Esmond, rather surprising his father with his acumen. Horace himself had never thought of it in such obvious terms.

'Exactly. Very good. Well, it's the same with money. The law of thermodynamics is true in banking. Money always flows from those who have it to those that haven't.'

Under the birch trees at the top of Breakneck Hill, Esmond stopped.

'I don't understand,' he said. 'If the rich are always giving money to the poor, why do the poor stay poor?'

'Because they spend the money of course,' said Horace irritably.

'But if the rich give away their money, they can't keep it – and if they don't keep it they can't stay rich,' Esmond objected.

Mr Wiley looked wistfully at a distant golfer and sighed. He did not play golf himself but he rather wished he had taken it up. The desire to hit something was almost overwhelming and a small white ball might just have served as a sufficient substitute for his son. Resisting this impulse, he instead did his best to smile and at the same time to answer Esmond. Not that he had a clue what to say. He was saved by a faintly religious upbringing.

'The poor are always with us,' he quoted.

'But why are they always with us?'

Mr Wiley tried to think of a good reason for repeating a statement he had never considered before in any depth. There hadn't been any need to. The poor didn't require his services as a bank manager or, if they did, couldn't afford them and the only person who might be described as being less than comfortably off in the neighbourhood the Wileys lived in was old Mrs Rugg, the cleaning lady, who came in twice a week to do the hoovering and the heavier housework and who extorted five pounds an hour for the privilege. Mr Wiley didn't think she had any reason to call herself poor. All the same, having started this train of argument, he had to continue it.

'The reason the poor are always with us,' he said, suddenly inspired, 'is that they don't save. They spend all their earnings as soon as they get them and naturally the rich, who are much more clever, which is why they became rich in the first instance, get their money back. It is a cyclical process and goes to prove my point. And now I'm going home for tea.'

It was on such inconclusive arguments about the second law of thermodynamics and a whole host of other topics that young Esmond acquired a sense of certainty. In fact, it was less a sense of certainty than the conviction that, while he would never be able to understand why things were the way they were, there was a fixity of purpose about them, and an unalterable quality about the nature of society that made understanding wholly unnecessary.

Actually, this was a fairly comforting conclusion, particularly for an adolescent subject not only to the unsettling effects of his own very faint sexual awakening, but also to the scorn of other boys and, worse still, girls for his name, his ears, his funny physique and his not-quite-abandoned tendency towards lurking, especially when under stress. The violence this contempt aroused in Esmond had been temporarily assuaged by his ferocious drumming and those devastating piano lessons, but that respite had been taken away from him.

Since Esmond's subsequent crude scribbles on the cloakroom wall failed to have any lasting effect on his mother's deplorably mawkish feelings for him which she so frequently expressed in public and at such length, he felt somewhat happier at the prospect of a world where understanding why things were the way they were was largely unnecessary if not impossible.

And so it was that having to choose between his mother's excruciating love for him and the feelings that that provoked in him, and more comprehensibly his father's restricted and unchanging views on just about everything, Esmond Wiley thought to model himself upon the latter. Thought being an inoperative word in the entire family's case, his attempt was bound to fail.

Chapter 5

Horace Wiley had in recent weeks developed some slight affection for his son – a boy who could provide him with the means of silencing so voluble a wife, even if this required obscene drawings in the downstairs toilet and the expense of replacing the plaster and redecorating the place, could not be all bad.

He even forgave him the appalling din of the drums. They had, after all, driven Horace from the house early enough in the morning to avoid the rush hour and provided him with a perfectly legitimate excuse for coming home late in the evening with his morale reinforced by a couple of large Scotches at the Gibbet & Goose, the local pub. And now that he came to think of it, Mrs Wiley's encounter with the Noise

Abatement Officer and the threat of being prosecuted had been no bad thing either. It had lessened Vera's sense of authority, as had the scandal of the 'growing' whatnot in the lavatory and Mrs Lumsden's account of her experience there.

In short, Horace Wiley had come to appreciate Esmond's destructive gifts, so far removed from his own cautious and fearful existence. His early revulsion at finding the lad who could, to all intents and purposes, be his double lurking about the place was replaced with a new warmth towards the boy, coupled with a deep admiration for his spirit.

And so it was that when these early signs of rebellion had dissipated themselves and a reformed Esmond instead began to model himself once again on his father, Mr Wiley's new-found fondness entirely evaporated.

Being himself was bad enough, and indeed Horace had always found looking at his face in the bathroom mirror while shaving an especially dispiriting experience. But then to look up from his plate of porridge at breakfast and see a younger version of himself, a dreadful replica, seated across the table duplicating his own actions and even eating porridge in the same way and with the same sort of reluctance – Vera insisted that porridge was the healthiest food for his heart – did nothing for his state of mind.

Or, for that matter, for his health. Never good, Horace Wiley's body now reacted to this mirror image of his youthful self, awash with burgeoning manhood, or manhood as burgeoning as one would expect from a burgeoning bank manager in Croydon, by plunging paradoxically into premature old age, as if to escape the torment of this unwanted recognition.

At forty-five, Horace Wiley looked sixty, and a year later had so much the appearance of a man of sixty-five that a visiting manager from the Lowland Bank's head office went so far as to enquire what he intended to do the next year when he retired. That evening, Mr Wiley returned from the Gibbet & Goose with six double Scotches inside him instead of the usual two.

'Of course I'm drunk,' he told his wife with some difficulty when she accused him. 'And you'd be drunk too if you could see yourself like I do.'

Mrs Wiley had been understandably furious.

'Don't you dare talk to me like that,' she shouted. 'You married me for better or for worse and it's not my fault I am not as beautiful as I once was.'

'True, very true,' said Horace who found the statement peculiar. He had never found her beautiful so he couldn't see why she should raise the issue now. Before he could puzzle this out and find a kitchen chair to slump into, she went on.

'You should take a look at yourself,' she snapped.

Horace peered at her and tried to focus. There appeared to be two of her.

'I do. All the time,' he muttered, making for the

chair. 'It's unbearable. It's awful. I can't escape looking at myself. I'm . . . he's always there. Always bloody there.'

It was his wife's turn to peer. She wasn't used to dealing with drunks and in any case she had never seen Horace more than mildly in his cups before. To have him come home in this awful condition only to insult her and then, slumped in a kitchen chair, to start talking about himself in the third person suggested more than mere drunkenness. Something more organic, perhaps even dementia, briefly crossed her mind before a whiff, in fact a veritable blast, of Scotch hit her as Horace struggled to his feet with an ashen face.

'There it is again,' he screamed staring wildly past her at the kitchen door. 'And now there are two of me. And what are they doing in my pyjamas?'

Mrs Wiley glanced apprehensively over her shoulder. She had DTs on her mind now. Perhaps Horace had been a secret drinker and the stuff had finally caught up with him, sending him crazy. But it was only Esmond, lurking. Before she could point out this seemingly obvious fact Horace started again.

'Out, damned spot! Out, I say!' he yelled, the overdose of Scotch evidently combining with vivid memories of a school trip to the Old Vic. 'One, two: why then, 'tis time to do it. Hell is murky!'

Grabbing a carving knife, Horace drunkenly advanced on his son, lunged at him and fell flat on his face.

'What's up with Dad?' Esmond asked, as Vera knelt by Horace and removed the knife.

'He's not himself,' she answered. 'Or he seems to think someone else is him. Or something. Leave off lurking, Esmond, and help get your father sorted before I ring for an ambulance.'

Together they dragged Horace up the stairs and put him to bed, by which time Vera had decided not to call the doctor after all. Instead she phoned her brother Albert who said he'd come over in the morning.

'But I need you now,' Vera insisted. 'Horace has just tried to stab Esmond. He's out of his mind.'

Albert kept his thoughts about his brother-in-law's mental condition to himself and put the phone down. He was over the alcohol limit himself and he had no intention of losing his licence for no better reason than that Horace Wiley had tried to do what any sane father would have done years ago.

Chapter 6

And so while Horace escaped from the torment of his family life in drunken sleep, his wife spent a sleepless night trying to come to terms with the knowledge that her husband was insane and that he would lose his job at the bank and end his days in a lunatic asylum which all the neighbours would know about. This combination of ghastly outcomes led her thoughts to an even more melodramatic conclusion: that Horace might actually succeed in murdering her darling son as soon as her back was turned. Vera Wiley determined never to leave them alone again, and so strong was her romantic imagination that she gained some comfort from the prospect of defending her darling Esmond even if this meant being stabbed to death herself by her demented husband in the process. Naturally, Horace would die with her – she would see to that – and Esmond would go through life suitably haunted by unrequited guilt (Vera wasn't sure what 'unrequited' meant except that it had something to do with love and was somehow unavoidable) and the dread secret of the tragedy which he could never bring himself to tell anyone. Vera accompanied these theatrical thoughts with a series of sobs and finally towards dawn dozed fitfully while her husband snored.

In his bedroom, Esmond listened to these sounds and tried to understand what had happened, and why his father had called him a 'damned spot' and told him to get the hell out of the house. It was most peculiar and, to an impressionable youth, deeply disturbing. And his father's intentions with regard to the use of the carving knife had been too obvious to be ignored.

Caught between an embarrassingly sentimental mother and a manifestly murderous father, or, at the very least, one who didn't behave at all rationally, it was not surprising that Esmond felt the need to escape into a healthier and less confusing atmosphere in which he wouldn't be accepted so uncritically by his mother and rejected so bitterly by his father. There were other worlds to conquer and the sooner he could find one that suited him the better. By the time he finally fell asleep Esmond, in his first act of rebellion since the ill-fated experiment with the drums, had made up his mind to run away from home. It was too bad. He shouldn't have to put up with such treatment and even if he ended up living on the streets, poor and hungry and friendless, it had to be better than this.

But he was saved this desperate measure by his Uncle Albert who arrived the next morning in his Aston Martin after Esmond had left for school.

'Now what's all this about?' he demanded in his usual loud voice as soon as he entered the house. Vera hurried him into the kitchen and shut the door.

'It's Horace. He came home drunk and started shouting at Esmond and then he grabbed a knife and tried to kill him. He said the most horrible things about me too and how there were two of him and – '

'Two what of him?' Albert interrupted.

'I don't know. He wasn't making any sense. He just said he was always looking at himself and he couldn't stand it any more.'

Albert considered this prospect and thought he understood.

'Can't say I blame him. Dreadful-looking fellow. Comes of being a bank manager. I've never known one who wasn't bloody sour. Can't think why you married the bloke.'

'Because he loved me passionately. He couldn't live without me,' said Vera, who had long since translated this fiction into fact. 'We got engaged . . . he proposed to me on Beachy Head and – '

'Yes, I know he did, don't I just,' said Albert, before he had to hear the story again. 'What I want to know is what you expect me to do about him now he's gone completely off his trolley. What does the doctor say?'

Vera sat down miserably at the kitchen table and shook her head.

'I haven't asked him. I mean, if I call the doctor he may say Horace is . . . well, not right in the head and he'd lose his job at the bank and then where would we be?'

'Where's Horace now?'

'He's upstairs in bed. I rang the bank and said he had a temperature and wouldn't be in for a day or two. Oh, Albert, I don't know what to do.' She paused and looked at the drawer where the carving knife was. 'I mean, next time I may not be around when he attacks Esmond.'

'Has he ever attacked him before?'

Vera shook her head.

'And what did Esmond say?'

'He just asked what was wrong with his dad.'

'You mean he hadn't said anything to annoy Horace?'

'He hadn't said a word. He'd just come down in his pyjamas to find out why Horace was shouting and carrying on about there being two of himself. The poor boy didn't get a chance to say anything before Horace grabbed the knife and hurled himself at him. It was horrible.'

'Must've been,' said Albert, who couldn't for the life of him imagine his brother-in-law doing anything so impetuous any more than he could imagine Horace proposing passionately to Vera at the top of Beachy Head. Bloody hell, he must have been as tight as an owl to go for Esmond with Vera in the room. Even Albert would have thought twice before getting across his sister.

'Still don't see what I can do about it,' he went on. 'I mean to say . . . well, my advice is to keep him away from the bottle.'

'You don't imagine for a moment I let him drink in the house?' said Vera indignantly. 'Because I most certainly don't. Only one glass of wine at Christmas but that's different.'

Again Albert had to reassess his brother-in-law's character.

'You're not telling me he gets tanked up in pubs? Horace in a pub? I don't believe it. Bank managers don't go anywhere near pubs. It's against their religion.'

'Well, he gets mad drunk somewhere, that I do know. He comes home smelling like a brewery. And he's always late. He gets up at the crack of dawn and comes home so late I have to put his supper in the oven. Anyway, you go up and have a talk with him. I want to know what's going on.'

Albert gave in. He might have been a formidable figure in the second-hand car trade in Essex but he'd never been able to stand up to his sister. He went upstairs and found Horace looking ghastly.

'Hullo, hullo,' he said loudly. 'What's all this I hear about you hitting the bottle and going for Esmond with a knife?'

Mr Wiley shrank down the bed. He couldn't bear his brother-in-law at the best of times, and now was the worst. He had a fearful headache and the horrors of the night were still with him. To be questioned by a man he firmly believed to be a criminal and probably some sort of gangland leader was the last straw.

'I don't know what you're talking about,' he murmured weakly. 'I haven't been well.'

'You don't have to tell me, Horace, you don't have to tell me,' said Albert and opened the curtains with a jerk.

Mr Wiley cowered under the bedclothes and moaned but his brother-in-law wasn't to be stopped. Albert was getting his own back for years of Horace's moral superiority. He sat down heavily on the bed and pulled the bedclothes off the sick man's face. In the bright sunlight Mr Wiley looked worse and felt worse still. Even Albert Ponson was shaken.

'Blimey,' he said. 'You've got something a bloody sight worse than a hangover, mate. And I don't mean maybe.'

'I know I have.'

'Know what it is?' Albert asked, almost sympathetically. This was deathbed stuff.

'Yes,' said Horace. 'I know all right.'

'Not the pox, is it?' Albert enquired. His mind ran along sordid lines.

'The pox?' said Horace whose mind didn't.

'Yeah, you know. The old tertiary. Syph or gonorrhoea.'

'Certainly not,' said Horace indignantly, momentarily startled out of his discomfort. 'What the hell do you think I am?'

'All right, all right. No need to get toffee-nosed about it. Only asking. Could happen to anyone.'

'Well, it couldn't happen to me,' said Horace, and subsided onto the pillow only slightly mollified.

Albert Ponson's next remark did him no good at all.

'All I'm saying is you look like you ought to book in with a good undertaker. I've seen blokes look better when they've turned off the life-support machine.'

Horace stared at him venomously.

'Thank you very much,' he said. 'You're a great comfort, you are. Now, if you don't mind, I'd be grateful if you'd go back downstairs and let me get some rest.'

But Albert wasn't to be budged so easily.

'Can't do that,' he said. 'Vera wants to know what's been going on, like. You're getting up early and coming home late stinking of booze – you got a piece on the side or something?'

'A piece? What do you mean by that?'

'A bird, a lover. You know, a floozy.'

'Well, you can go down and tell her I haven't,' said Horace. 'It's nothing like that.'

Albert looked at him doubtfully.

'All right, I'll believe you, though millions wouldn't. It's not the big C, is it?'

'No, it isn't. It isn't anything physical. It's much worse than that.'

He stopped. Albert Ponson wasn't the sort of person he wanted to confide in. When it came to understanding the problems of having a son like Esmond lurking around the place and looking exactly like you and behaving exactly like you, then Albert would be no help at all. A man who went around giving drums to tone-deaf nephews had to be wholly lacking in sensibility.

On the other hand, Horace couldn't bring himself to explain his feelings to Vera. Her combination of devotion to Esmond and horrible sentimentality, which Horace had come to recognise as another form of sadism, or at least violence, made his confession impossible. Anything might be better than the appalling scene that would result from even the hint that Horace couldn't stand the sight of his son. Albert was sufficiently cowed by his sister to understand that. Horace came to a sudden decision.

'It's Esmond. That's what's the matter with me. He's doing terrible things to my psyche.'

Albert Ponson tried to come to grips with the statement. Being in the pre-used car business he knew about psychology, but psyche was a new one to him.

'You mean with those drums? Yeah, well, Vera told me about that and all, but – '

'Not the drums,' said Horace. 'And not the piano practice either. It's him . . .' He sighed miserably. 'You don't have a family so you wouldn't know.'

'No, Belinda and me haven't been blessed with kids,' Albert said stiffly. It was evidently a sore point.

'Blessed? Blessed? You don't know how lucky you are.'

'I wouldn't put it like that myself. I mean, we've been trying for years. Something has to be wrong with Belinda's insides because it sure as hell isn't me . . . Anyway, what's wrong with Esmond? Seems a fine strapping lad to me.'

Horace momentarily forgot his hangover. It had never occurred to him that anyone could regard Esmond as a fine strapping anything, and that 'lad' was definitely suspicious.

'You're lying,' he said. 'Fine he isn't, and strapping he's certainly not. He's the spitting image of me at his age and that's not something I'd wish on my own worst enemy. I can't stand him and never want to have to look at his pathetic face again.'

Albert Ponson stared at Horace and tried to come to terms with this extraordinary statement. He had never found his brother-in-law in the least likeable and hadn't for a moment understood why Vera had married the fellow, but he shared his sister's simple sentimentality and belief in the crudest of family values. In his world fathers were supposed to love their sons or at least be proud of them. It was the same with cats and dogs. You liked them because they were yours. To go around saying you detested your own son wasn't just not nice – it was unnatural.

'That's not a nice thing to say, Horace,' he said finally. 'Not nice at all. Esmond's your son. It's only right and proper he looks like you. It would be bloody odd if he didn't. I mean to say, if I had a son and he looked like someone else, I wouldn't be too happy, me being away from home so often, know what I mean?'

Horace thought he did but he kept his thoughts to himself. He had begun to have a most remarkable idea. It required his brother-in-law's cooperation, though it would have to be unwitting. He would have to act very carefully indeed. Horace Wiley fell back on his experience as a bank manager. For more years than he cared to remember he had lured customers who least required overdrafts into accepting them, while refusing loans to small businesses that desperately did need them.

'Well, I agree it's not right to feel the way I do. I know that, but I can't help myself. He's always hanging around, imitating me. It's . . . it's like having a doppelgänger.'

'A doppelgänger?' said Albert, who had as much trouble with the word as he'd had with psyche, perhaps understandably given that his mind seldom left the world of buying and selling cars. And he'd certainly never heard of one called a doppelgänger.

'A double, someone who's always with you and acts the same way as you do and you can't get rid of him,' Horace explained. He paused with a sinister glint in his eyes. 'Except by killing him.'

'Blimey,' said Albert, now thoroughly alarmed. Horace was clearly as mad as a hatter. 'Are you telling me you want to murder him?'

'Not want to. Got to. You don't know what it's like never being able to get away from someone who's just like you but isn't. If only he'd go away for a bit and leave me alone I'd feel a lot safer. I mean, it's not nice getting this terrible urge to murder your own son. And I've got Vera to think of. I'd leave the bank and go away myself if it would do any good, but I've got to support her and earn a living and she's been such a wonderful wife I wouldn't want to do anything to upset her.'

Albert Ponson considered the statement and found it difficult to reconcile with Horace's dreadful urge to kill Esmond. 'Upset' was putting it mildly. Vera's reaction would be far more deadly. In fact, 143 Selhurst Road would go down in the annals of British crime history along with Rillington Place and other houses where there'd been multiple horrors. It wouldn't do Ponson's Pre-Used Motors much good either.

Seeing Albert weaken, Horace struck again.

'I've thought of how to do it too. I'd have to get

rid of every trace of him of course,' he said. 'I couldn't have bits of him in the garden for instance, or under the cellar floor. So I'd have to dissolve his body in acid. I measured the water butt behind the garage and he'd fit in there easily, lanky limbs and all, and I've got a customer at the bank in the acid and chemical business who'd let me have forty gallons of nitric acid cheap.'

Albert sat down at the foot of the bed with his head in his hands, only half listening to his brother-in-law's ravings, and all hope of beating a hasty exit back to the relative sanity of the Ponson bungalow disappeared.

Chapter 7

By the time Albert Ponson went downstairs, he was a shaken man. His feelings for his brother-in-law had turned from contempt to detestation and fear. The bloody man had described his plans for disposing of Esmond's remains with a wealth of detail and relish that had been wholly convincing. Horace Wiley might be a bank manager but he was also on the verge of becoming a homicidal maniac. To add to this impression of lunacy, he had interspersed the description of the acid-bath technique with repeated remarks about loving his wife and worrying about her feelings.

Albert Ponson shared his concerns. The thought of marching into the kitchen and telling Vera that her damned husband had measured the water butt behind the garage with a view to putting her son in it and adding fifteen gallons of concentrated nitric acid to it made his blood run cold.

'It's a big butt but with Esmond in it I don't think I'll need more than twenty gallons,' Horace had said. 'I can always top it up a bit later when most of the body is dissolved. And since there's a lid on it, no one would dream of looking for him in there. That would be the last place they'd look, don't you think?'

Albert Ponson had hardly been able to think at all. The most he could do was mutter, 'I don't believe what I'm hearing,' over and over again. But now, as he stood hesitantly outside the kitchen door, he thought furiously and arrived at a conclusion. Vera wouldn't like it, but she'd have to lump it. It would be preferable to losing Esmond in an acid butt.

'I've had a good long talk with Horace,' he told her. 'And what he needs is complete rest if he's to avoid a nervous breakdown. And obviously having Esmond around the house all the time is part of the problem.'

'But he's not around the house all the time. He's at school. And anyway, even if he was, Horace isn't here to be bothered. He's at the bank. Or the pub. He leaves here at the crack of dawn and then comes home drunk and – '

'Yes, I know all that,' Albert interrupted. 'But that's because Esmond . . . that's one of Horace's symptoms. He's suffering from . . . well, from stress.'

'Stress? What sort of stress? And what about me?

64

You don't think I'm under stress with an alcoholic husband who comes home and tries to kill my only son with a carving knife and – '

'I know. I know you are,' Albert interrupted again, desperate not to get into a discussion about Horace's murderous tendencies. Carving knives were mild compared to water butts filled with nitric acid.

'The point is that Horace needs . . .' He paused and searched for a word. 'He needs space. He's got a midlife crisis.'

'A midlife crisis?' said Vera doubtfully.

'Yeah, like . . . like he's got the male menopause. Now what's wrong?'

Vera had snorted in a most unpleasant manner.

'Male menopause, my foot,' she said bitterly. 'He's had that ever since I married him. He didn't have to wait till midlife to come up with male menopauses. If you knew what I've had to put up with the last sixteen years. If you only knew . . .'

But Albert didn't want to know. He wasn't a squeamish man, or even a faintly sensitive one, but there were some things he definitely didn't want to hear about and his sister's sex life was one of them.

'Look,' he said. 'You asked me down here to talk to Horace and sort things out, and that's what I'm trying to do. And what I'm saying is that Horace is on the verge of a major breakdown. Now, if you want him to lose his job and go on the dole and have him sitting at home in front of the telly – ' He stopped, an idea suddenly coming into his mind. ' – that is, if you've still got a telly what with all the debts he's piled up . . .'

The idea of Horace having debts galvanised Vera just as Albert knew it would. Sentimental she might be but she was still a Ponson and money mattered to her.

'Oh God,' she said. This was even worse than she'd thought. 'Don't tell me he's gone and got us into debt as well as everything else. He's been gambling, hasn't he? First the drink and then the violence and now this. Oh, Albert, what are we going to do?'

Albert took out a handkerchief and mopped his forehead. He'd known mentioning money and debts would send Vera up the wall. But, as he'd expected, it was making her listen to him a lot more carefully.

'The first thing is to get him back to work,' he said. 'His debts aren't the main problem, although what possessed him to put all your money into stocks and shares I'll never know. Never mind that, they say the stock market is on the upturn and once he's back at work he can get it all sorted out. Now, what he really needs is time and space from Esmond. If not, there's no saying what the consequences may be.'

'But the school holidays are coming up at the end of the week and how can I stop my own darling Esmond from getting on Horace's nerves? He's such a lovely boy and always wants to be helpful and – '

'I've thought of that,' said Albert before she could

go into her nauseous sentimental mode. 'Esmond can come and help me around the garage and give Horace a bit of peace and quiet to get well again . . .'

Upstairs Horace Wiley listened to the murmur of voices in the kitchen and felt better. That bit about the water butt had done the trick. Even Albert had gone a funny colour when he'd heard that one.

Chapter 8

In the Ponsons' extensive bungalow, a confection of flock wallpaper, gold Dralon sofas and ankle-deep pink carpets, and where every bedroom had both a bathroom and a jacuzzi, the news that the place was shortly to be infested by Esmond Wiley was not entirely welcome.

Belinda Ponson, Albert's wife, was not a large, loud, effulgent woman like her sister-in-law and she was certainly not a sentimental one. She was best described as quiet and particular – although she had not always been that way – and she was particularly particular about her furnishings. The thought of what an adolescent with muddy shoes and oily hands would do to the flock wallpaper and the Dralon sofas, not to mention the pink carpet, deeply disturbed her.

'I'm not having him spoil the decor', she told Albert, who always had to take his shoes off in the front porch and put on some special slippers before entering the bungalow. 'I know what boys are like. That sister of yours has spoilt that son of hers something awful and he's bound to be unhygienic as well. All boys are. What possessed you to invite him without consulting me?'

'Horace did,' Albert said tersely. 'He's off his rocker.'

'I don't care what he's off. He's never done you any favours so why have you got to do him any? That's what I want to know.'

'Because, like I say, he's off his trolley, and he'll stay off it and worse if he has the boy around the house. I don't want Vera on my hands for the rest of her natural. Do you want her living here and interfering and all?'

There was no need for Belinda to answer.

'Well, all I can say is I'm not having Esmond bring his girlfriends here and lounging about in dirty jeans and messing my house up.'

Albert helped himself to a large Scotch from a cut-glass decanter with a gold-plated label that said Chivas Regal.

'He doesn't wear jeans. He goes around in a blue suit and a tie just like his dad,' he said. 'That's what's driven Horace bonkers. Says it's like having another him around the house.'

'Another him? What are you talking about? I never heard such nonsense in my life.'

'Like he's got a dopple . . . a double. Like he's a split personality. And seeing Horace is the way he is, I mean the way he looks, it must be bloody horrible to have two of him round the house.'

'If that's the case, I don't want one of him,' said Belinda. 'Your sister can keep all three of them.'

'Three of them? What the hell are you on about?' Albert demanded. But Belinda had already gone through to the Poggenpohl kitchen to relieve her feelings on the washing machine.

Around her the appurtenances of modern living had their usual soothing, emollient effect. They almost disguised her feelings from herself. The blender, the microwave, the split-level oven with revolving spit, the espresso machine and the stainless-steel sink with the separate spigot from the reverse osmosis water filter, all served to assure her that she had some sort of purpose and meaning in life when life with Albert often suggested the opposite.

Albert could have his swimming bath and his leather-padded bar with its saddled and stirruped stools and Wild West number plates and flags – and even his Yellow Rose of Texas bumper sticker; he could have his barbecues and gas-fired charcoal grills to impress his friends and prove his manliness; in fact, he could have everything he wanted – except her kitchen and her secret thoughts. And her unsatisfied desire. Although come to think of it, he could have her unsatisfied desire if only he'd satisfy it. No, the kitchen was sacrosanct if it only masked other needs.

Belinda Ponson mused about Esmond Wiley's coming. If he really was like his father and wore a blue suit and a tie he might be just the antidote to Albert she had been waiting for. Albert was too obvious and too crude. And he'd failed to give her what she wanted above anything else in the world. A daughter. Something she had dreamed of since she was a little girl herself, surrounded by grandmas and aunties and cousins.

Belinda brightened. Perhaps the lad could be something else. Like a toy boy. She knew for a fact that Albert hadn't been faithful to her over all the years of their marriage and perhaps this was the very moment to break free of the wretched man.

If Esmond was like his father then odds were that he would be timorous and biddable and easily influenced. In fact, the more Belinda thought about it the more pleasing the idea of having Esmond around the house became.

Chapter 9

Almost precisely the opposite thoughts were going through Vera Wiley's mind.

Vera still hadn't got over the shock of hearing that Horace had got into debt by gambling on the stock market. She couldn't bear to think of the consequences this would have if he didn't recover from his breakdown and get back to his desk at the bank and sell whatever shares he still had that would go up when the market rose again.

On the other hand, the prospect of parting even temporarily with her love child Esmond appalled her. Especially having him go to that cow of a sister-in-law, Belinda. Albert was all right in his own bluff way, even if his business was a bit dodgy, but that Belinda wasn't a nice person at all.

'If I've said it once I've said it a thousand times,' she told Horace without exaggeration, 'that Belinda is a cold fish. What Albert sees in her I can't think.'

Horace could, but he kept his thoughts on the subject to himself. Albert's choice of an expert property lawyer and tax consultant as his bride had been a shrewd one for a man in his line of business in Essex, even if Belinda had apparently retired from the profession on marriage. In his own devious heart, Horace rather envied him. Besides, Belinda was a good-looking woman and had kept her figure, which was more than could be said for Vera. And even more to his liking was that she kept herself to herself, at least when there was company. She was just there in the background, making herself useful in the kitchen and not hogging the limelight like Vera and Albert.

Not that the Wileys had been invited to many of the Ponsons' parties, and the ones they had gone to had been too rowdy for Horace's taste and his reputation as a respectable bank manager. And by all accounts they had been tame affairs compared to some Albert had boasted about. Even Vera had been shocked by her brother's accounts of mixed couples in jacuzzis, though Horace had privately suspected her of a good deal of envy. Which made it all the more surprising that she was prepared to let Esmond go and stay at Ponson Place for the summer.

Horace lay in bed, nursing his hangover and resisting the urge to cover his ears as Vera rattled on. He wondered what the hell Albert had told her that had been so persuasive. Obviously he hadn't mentioned the water butt behind the garage. Vera would have gone out of her mind with rage. But instead she was harping on about what a cold fish that Belinda was, and not being sure about Esmond being happy with going away to Essex. And how would a woman who couldn't have children of her own know how to feed a growing boy like Esmond? Esmond was so fussy about his food and besides he was delicate and . . .

Horace listened to her and tried to look even sicker than he felt. As far as he was concerned, Belinda Ponson could starve his ghastly son to death or make his life utter hell as long as she didn't drive the brute to come home.

'I just need to rest,' he whimpered, partly as an answer to his own unspoken thoughts, and was relieved to hear Vera sigh and most surprisingly agree, without the added comment that if he would come home stinking drunk he'd got what he deserved. Instead she went downstairs and waited for Esmond to come home from school to tell him that Uncle Albert and Auntie Belinda had very kindly asked him to stay for the summer holidays.

All the same, Vera's doubts remained. Something was wrong and that something hadn't anything to do with Horace getting drunk or coming home late and talking about Esmond being him. It wasn't even the inconceivable idea of Horace gambling on the stock market. There was something else niggling away at her.

Sitting at the kitchen table with Sackbut staring out the window from his customary place by the cactus, it slowly dawned on her what that something might be. And if she was right, then Horace's behaviour, odd and mad as it had seemed, was actually calculated and purposeful and made complete sense. What if Horace had another woman or, as the romances she read put it, a mistress? That would explain everything, his leaving the house early and coming home later and later, his drinking and how he'd got into debt. It even explained his horrid behaviour to Esmond; he hated him because Esmond was a constant reminder of his duty as a father and a husband. And of course it explained why he was no good in bed and she'd always had to do all the lovemaking.

As this terrible conviction hit her and she knew herself to be a wronged woman, nay, a betrayed wife, and Horace no more than a philanderer, conflicting tidal waves of emotion crashed over her. Her first impulse, to rush upstairs and confront the faithless Horace with his guilt, was succeeded by the thought of the effect on her darling Esmond. The poor lad would be traumatised.

It wasn't a word that came at all easily to a woman who lived an emotional life almost entirely based on early-nineteenth-century Regency bucks who crushed maidens to their manly breasts, fought duels after dancing till dawn and then rode great black horses post-haste, etc., but she'd heard it on the telly and it came to her now.

She couldn't allow Esmond to be traumatised. She had to do her duty as a mother, and if that meant sacrificing her own feelings, at least for the time being, she would do so. Which didn't mean she wasn't going to express her fury the moment Esmond had left for Ponson Place. Oh, she'd have something to say to Horace then . . .

She was stopped by another thought: the cunning and skill with which Horace had managed to get Esmond out of the house. He had said something to Albert, something that had so shocked that bluff man that Albert had come down to the kitchen clearly shaken to the core by what he had just heard. Vera had never seen her brother so ashen and Albert was not a man to be shocked easily.

Of course, of course, Horace had confessed everything to him. Albert had forced Horace to tell him everything about the other woman who haunted his dreams. Or Horace had boasted to Albert about his mistress who exhausted him nightly, which is why he was always late home with nothing left for Vera, his loyal wife.

For a moment Vera's fury nearly sent her dashing up to the bedroom to have it out but the combination of

Esmond being traumatised and the feeling that she had more to gain by pretending to know nothing prevented her. Instead, she went out into the garden and sauntered tragically among the pink aubretia, the pelargoniums so red and the trailing lobelias so very, very blue. Here, among the bedding plants and the striped and weed-free lawn, she could weep unseen those tears her new role required.

In fact, her performance did not go unseen. Horace watched her from the bedroom and was puzzled. He had grown accustomed to her theatricals and sudden changes of mood, so in the present circumstances he would have expected something more melodramatic and vigorous than this pensive and melancholy performance. A woman wailing for her demon lover or, in the present case, a mother wailing for her demon son seemed more appropriate than this demure and mournful progress. A new sense of unease crept over him. He'd desperately like to know what that damned oaf Albert had told her. It must have been something perfectly frightful to put her in this melancholy. Horace turned over and tried to sleep.

Chapter 10

By the time Esmond arrived home from school, his mother had played out her role. It wasn't sufficiently active to sustain for very long, and besides, she was determined to be bright and cheerful so that her darling boy wouldn't be traumatised.

'Daddy's much better today,' she announced, as she made tea and toast with honey. 'He's been working ever so hard lately and he needs to rest so we've got to be quiet and not disturb him.'

'I am quiet,' said Esmond. 'I've been quiet ever since I gave up the drums and the piano lessons ages ago.'

'Yes, dear, you've been very good. It's just that Daddy's nerves aren't very . . . well, he's exhausted himself mentally.'

'You mean he's been drinking,' said Esmond, with rather more insight into his father's problem than Mrs Wiley liked. She preferred her Esmond to be innocent.

'I know all about it, Mum. He goes to the Gibbet & Goose and sits there drinking double Scotches when he gets off the train every night.'

Vera was appalled, though less by the fact than by Esmond's understanding.

'He doesn't. I mean, he may do occasionally, but . . . Anyway, how do you know?'

'Because Rosie Bitchall told me. Her dad's the barman there.'

'Rosie Bitchall? That horrid girl who came to your seventeenth birthday party and went behind the sofa with Richard? You don't still see her?'

Vera was genuinely agitated now.

'She's in my class and we're going to the same college next year.'

Vera stopped pouring tea and put the pot down. Esmond's simple statement had decided her. She had no intention of allowing her only son to fall in love with a slut like Rosie Bitchall who wore a ring through her nose and who, to put it mildly, was no better than she should be and who, in the words of Mrs Blewett, was a chip off the old block, the old block in question being her mother, Mabel. Vera knew exactly what that meant.

'Well, Rosie Bitchall must have been mistaken.

Anyway, enough of that. Your Uncle Albert came here to see Daddy this morning,' she said, 'and he and Auntie Belinda have invited you to stay with them until Daddy's better. Now, isn't that nice of them?'

'Yes, but – '

Mrs Wiley wasn't having any 'buts'.

'I'm not going to argue about it,' she said. 'I'm not having you rampage about the house with your father lying upstairs ill in bed. And besides, you'll learn something useful from your Uncle Albert.'

'I don't want to become a second-hand car dealer,' said Esmond stubbornly. 'I want to go into a bank like Dad and make money.'

This was too much for Mrs Wiley. It swept aside the last vestiges of her romanticism. She'd rather Esmond became a rogue – a dashing rogue naturally – than a bank manager like Horace.

'If you think . . . if you think your father makes money being a bank manager . . . well, let me tell you that Albert makes four times as much as your father. He's a rich man is Uncle Albert. Whoever heard of a rich bank manager?' She paused and found another argument. 'Besides, your uncle will give you a reference and they were saying only the other day that what young people need nowadays is work experience. Having work experience does you more good than anything else.'

Which didn't help to persuade Esmond. Caught between his mother's public adulation and his father's rejection, a rejection that had reached the point where he had tried to stab him with a carving knife in a drunken frenzy, he was now to be subjected to his Uncle Albert who was as embarrassing to be with as his mother was. And who was, as his father had said repeatedly, as crooked as any second-hand car dealer who ever welded two insurance write-offs into one single-owned Cavalier. To add to that, he lived in Essex.

In any case, his mother's reaction to the mention of Rosie Bitchall had so obviously supposed he was in love with her that it made him cringe and squirm with disgust. He wasn't in the least interested in the wretched Rosie. In fact, he was unique among his peers in being rather revolted than attracted by the whole notion of sex.

This was Esmond's wake-up call. The only good thing to have come out of the past twenty-four hours was that it had given him important things to think about, primarily the obvious need to avoid being anything like his parents. After years in which he had done his utmost to fulfil their conflicting expectations for him and had so obviously failed, he was now determined to be himself. Who that self was he had no idea, or only vague and fleeting ones. As a boy he had been subject to a host of temporary impulses that came and went of their own accord and over which he had absolutely no control. One moment he was going to be a poet – his mother's fondness for

Tennyson's 'The Splendour Falls on Castle Walls' and the fact that as a child she'd overdosed him on Rupert Bear had given him the gift of scansion and the curse of automatic rhyme – then a few minutes later the contrary impulse to be a bulldozer driver and smash his way through hedges and generally destroy things had swept poetry aside. He had once seen a demolition team on television bring an enormous factory chimney crashing to the ground by removing bricks at the base which they had replaced with wood and had then set fire to, and the idea of being such a demolition expert fleetingly appealed to him. It spoke to something within him in much the same way his drum-beating had: it expressed the violence of his emotions and his overwhelming desire to assert himself somehow. Unfortunately, he had no sooner arrived at this notion of selfhood than it too was swept aside by the feeling that he had been put on earth to do something more important and constructive than blow up chimneys and demolish things.

And now becoming a bank manager had lost its appeal for him too. Not if it meant getting up at six in the morning and coming home drunk after nine at night and not even making as much money as Uncle Albert. His future had to hold something better than that.

For the first time in his life Esmond had begun to think for himself.

Chapter 11

At the end of the week, after enduring many sleepless nights, Vera drove Esmond to her brother's flash bungalow near Colchester, all the way stressing the importance of behaving properly and not telling Auntie Belinda about Daddy getting drunk and trying to attack him with the carving knife.

'That's something nobody but us must ever know about,' she said. 'As you know, your father's been under a lot of strain lately. And don't go around telling them he's had a nervous breakdown either. The least said the soonest mended.'

Esmond promised he wouldn't say anything but he kept his real thoughts to himself.

They mainly centred round the prospect of living

in the same house as his Aunt Belinda. That morning he'd overheard his father say that, while he disapproved of Uncle Albert's vulgarity and dodgy second-hand car business, he was at least partly human which wasn't something that could be said for that fucking termagant of a wife of his. It was about the only time Esmond had heard Horace use that swear word and, having not understood what a termagant was and having had to find its meaning in a dictionary, he wasn't looking forward to his stay with her.

Mr Wiley had also called her a harridan, a virago and a shrew. Once again Esmond had recourse to the dictionary and had come away with an even more terrifying impression of Aunt Belinda, made worse by his mother's agreement that what his father had said was perfectly true. But from his own experience, going on what little he'd seen of his aunt on the very infre-quent visits the Ponsons had made to the Wileys, she had seemed quite good-looking, if a bit snooty and quiet.

All in all, the drive had done nothing to give Esmond any confidence in his future – if he had one, which was starting to seem unlikely. Mrs Wiley's driving, ever-erratic, had been made positively lethal by the impending loss of her son for however short a time and, less importantly, the conviction that Horace was a murderous and philandering lunatic who would have to be placed in a mental hospital. Vera had come down to the kitchen that morning to find her husband sharpening carving knives – 'honing' would have been a more accurate word – until they had blades as dangerous as old-fashioned cut-throat razors. And then after breakfast – a difficult, largely silent affair – she'd caught him in the bathroom, his face covered in lather and evidently about to shave with the knife that had previously been reserved for Sunday roasts and special occasions. She had dragged it away from him, cutting her hand in the process, and had been horrified by the gleeful expression on his face and insane laughter that came from the bedroom when she had forced him back there and locked the door.

Having taken the precaution of keeping his door locked as much as possible and of sleeping in the spare bedroom, she had been alarmed to hear Horace pacing the floor nightly and then laughing maniacally. As a result her sleep had been disturbed to the point where she frequently fell asleep at the kitchen table after getting Esmond his breakfast and then hurrying him out of the house with some money for his lunch and orders not to come home until seven in the evening. All this nodding off meant that, to add to her problems, she was unable to read any of her romances in a leisurely fashion or even on a daily basis. She'd scarcely even been able to risk leaving the house to go shopping. Returning home from a quick trip to the corner shop on Thursday, she found that the window cleaner had arrived to do inside and out. To her horror, there stood Horace, still in his pyjamas, standing where the bottom of the man's ladder had been. Horace had let the ladder fall and now seemed to be closely examining the water butt at the back of the house, oblivious to the window cleaner's demands that he put the ladder back so he could get down and on with his work.

'For God's sake, get him to put the ladder back up,' the window cleaner yelled. 'I've been stuck up here in your bedroom for forty minutes and I've got fifteen more houses to do today. That bloody man . . .'

Mrs Wiley grabbed Horace and dragged him into the house and up to the bedroom. She unlocked the door, shoved him inside and let the man out. That done, she had made herself what in normal circumstances she'd have called 'a nice cup of tea' and tried to think. At least Esmond was going to the Ponsons' and obviously she would have to . . . No, she couldn't let a psychiatrist see Horace. He'd lose his job at the bank if he was sent to a loony bin or even if it got out that he had had a nervous breakdown. Loony bin was not the politically correct term she'd have used in polite society but in Horace's case it seemed entirely appropriate; he was loony.

So with these thoughts turbulently rising in what there was left of her own mind, it was hardly surprising that her driving was even more dangerously erratic than usual, leaving Esmond in a state of nervous exhaustion and terror.

By the time they reached the Ponsons' bungalow

he was practically speechless. They were greeted by Uncle Albert, bubbling with false bonhomie. In the background, Belinda was far less enthusiastic, eventually offering them tea in a tone of voice that suggested it was the last thing she wanted to offer.

'Now come on in and make yourselves at home,' said Albert, but Vera was too upset to accept.

'I've simply got to get home to poor Horace. He's in a dreadful state,' she said, and clasping Esmond to her ample bosom promptly burst into tears. Then, tearing herself away and kissing Esmond, much to his embarrassment, on his lips, she turned away from her darling boy and a moment later was driving back to Croydon and to her evidently demented husband.

Chapter 12

In Vera's absence, Horace had had a marvellous day. She had been so distraught at the prospect of losing her darling son to that awful Belinda that she had forgotten to take the key to the bedroom out of the door and Horace had managed to push it through onto a sheet of newspaper and pull this into the bedroom. Five minutes later he had found his razor in the bathroom where Vera had hidden it. He shaved and then, dressed in his best suit and carrying a hastily packed suitcase, he locked the door of the bedroom, pocketed the key and hurriedly left the house with a smile on his face.

It was more than a smile; it was a look of triumph. For the first time since his marriage, Horace Wiley felt a free man, a new man, a man with none of the ghastly emotional encumbrances his bloody wife had foisted onto him.

Spending the week in bed feigning madness – walking the floor at night and laughing maniacally whenever he thought Vera might be listening – had given him time to think. He'd decided that, finally, enough was enough. He was done with Vera, with her horrible relatives and with his lurking beast of a son. He wasn't going back to his job at the bank. He didn't need the salary now that he had escaped his responsibilities. For years he had been putting money into a private pension fund and an even larger amount he'd made on the stock market into a numbered account in Switzerland, both without telling his damnable wife. From now on she could fend for herself and for her wretched son.

Horace strode down Selhurst Road and, finding himself passing the Swan & Sugar Loaf, a pub he'd never frequented and where he wouldn't be recognised, went in and ordered a large whisky by way of celebration.

Horace took his drink to an empty corner and considered his next move. It was going to be a radical one. Going abroad was the obvious answer: Vera would never imagine him doing that. She was too scared of flying and until this moment he hadn't been too keen on it himself. But now he was a free man, a new man, he no longer cared how he travelled, only that he got as far away as possible.

Because of their fear of flying the Wileys had never been abroad, and Horace realised that his first priority was to get a passport. He wasn't at all certain, now he came to think about it, just how one went about it but he had an awful feeling that it involved filling in lots of forms and having photographs signed by doctors or fellow bank managers. He was sure that he had had to sign, in an official capacity, a photograph of a very dodgy-looking Jenkins when the junior clerk had been off to Amsterdam on his stag do. Horace wouldn't even be able to take the first step of getting a photograph taken quickly since it was Saturday and the post office where there was a photo booth was closed in the afternoon.

For a while Horace was crestfallen at this early curtailment of his plans but he brightened up when a fresh idea struck him. Finishing his whisky, he went down to the bank, unlocked the door and cut off the alarm system before entering. Once inside he locked the door again and unlocked the safe containing the personal documents etc. of the clients. It took over an hour to sift through the various last wills and testaments, ancient Premium Bonds and frayed and faded love letters stored in the safety-deposit boxes, but finally he found a passport with a photograph which bore at least a passing resemblance to him. It was perhaps less than ideal that it was held in the name of one Mr Ludwig Jansens who had been born in Jelgava some seventy years previously but the toll recent events had taken on Horace's looks meant that in a dim light it might do.

Having finished and locked the door once more, he set the alarm and went further along the high street where he caught a bus to the station on East Road. Two hours later, he was happily installed in an expensive hotel in London under his new false name. From now on he was going to treat himself well, and besides, it was the last place Vera would look for him.

That night Horace had an excellent dinner and got uproariously drunk to celebrate his freedom.

The next morning he had breakfast in his hotel bedroom trying to think how he could escape Britain without leaving any evidence of his ultimate destination. It would have to be in Europe. He now had a passport but that could be recorded if he tried to get into somewhere like America and his whereabouts subsequently traced. He would be safe enough once he was in the EU. There were no records of frontier crossings between Italy and France or Germany for that matter.

Horace still wasn't sure where he would hide from that dreadful wife he had so insanely married. And from the son he had obviously conceived, and whose mirror image had driven him to drink and, almost, to madness. It was only when he went down to settle his bill that he was inspired by an article in a newspaper on a side table. It mentioned Latvia belonging to the European Union. It was meant to be. Why on earth hadn't Ludwig's passport made him think of Latvia in the first place? It was perfect. From there he could get into Poland and then into Germany or anywhere else leaving no trail behind him.

Horace paid the hotel in cash and went to a travel agency where he explained that he had a phobia about flying and wanted instead to travel by boat to Latvia.

'The boats to Latvia are not liners. They are essentially steamers carrying cargo,' the clerk told Horace.

'Why are they called tramp steamers?'

'I've always thought it's because they're so slow. And I have to warn you that the passenger accommodation is nothing to write home about.'

Horace was about to say that writing home was the last thing he was going to do, but kept his thoughts to himself. He booked a passage and paid for it, then went out into the street with his documents. He was particularly pleased that the clerk had merely glanced at his passport and had written the wrong name down. Things were going well.

Chapter 13

Vera's feelings were the exact opposite to those of Horace. To say she was unhappy would be the understatement of far more than a year. She'd never been so desperately miserable in her life and of course she blamed Horace. If he hadn't gone off his head she wouldn't have had to send her love child to stay with that dreadful Belinda. She had never liked the woman and even before the wedding she had told Albert he had fallen for a hard and bitter gold-digger who would treat him like dirt. But he'd ignored her warning and look where it had got him: he was completely under her thumb to the point where, he told her, Belinda made him take his shoes off before he entered the house when he came home from work to prevent him making the thick carpet dirty.

By the time she had driven back through the evening rush-hour traffic – 'crawled' was a more precise word – accompanied by the shouts of furious drivers to 'move on, you stupid bitch', Vera was exhausted emotionally and physically. She dropped into a kitchen chair, put her head on the table and burst into tears. Finally she fell asleep, waking two hours later to find the sun had set and she was in darkness.

Vera turned the light on and although she wondered whether she should go upstairs to check on Horace she decided against it. This was all his fault. If he hadn't become an alcoholic none of this would have happened. He could go without his supper. He could go without his breakfast too for all she cared. Horrible, horrible man to have driven away her sweet boy.

Vera wasn't hungry herself but all the same she knew she had to keep her strength up. She opened a tin of baked beans and made some toast and having eaten them went upstairs to her room and bed.

Just before she dropped off it did occur to her that the bedside lamp in Horace's bedroom wasn't on. Well, he was probably asleep. Whatever he was, she didn't care. All her thoughts, such as they were, centred on her darling son.

Chapter 14

Vera need not have bothered. Esmond was having a wonderful time. Belinda had proved to be much more friendly than he had been led to expect.

Soon after his arrival, Belinda had insisted that Esmond change out of his blue suit and into something more comfortable – and, quickly realising that casual clothes were evidently not part of Esmond's wardrobe, she'd loaned him a pair of Albert's tracksuit bottoms. They looked a trifle odd teamed with Esmond's customary shirt and tie, but he had to admit that they were very comfortable indeed.

Belinda had then shown him how to use the jacuzzi. Esmond had never seen a jacuzzi before and thought it looked very exciting, although he had been a little embarrassed by Aunt Belinda's enthusiasm when she started to take her clothes off and get in to demonstrate how it worked properly, and he politely declined the invitation to join her in it.

In fact, everything about the bungalow seemed both exciting and wonderfully modern to him. His bedroom had a television in it and even a small espresso machine for making coffee. And just outside, he could see a large kidney-shaped swimming pool. In short, Ponson Place was as luxurious as anything he'd ever seen and decked out with stuff which was quite unlike the dull furniture at 143 Selhurst Road.

By the time Esmond came back to the sitting room with a still-rather-damp Belinda he had made up his mind that he was going to enjoy staying with the Ponsons. Uncle Albert had just poured himself a large Scotch.

'Have a drink,' he said. 'What's your poison?'

Esmond hesitated. He'd never heard the expression before.

'Poison?' he asked.

'What do you want to drink, lad?'

'I think I'll have a Coke.'

'Haven't got any. Try a good malt,' said his uncle and, without waiting for an answer, handed Esmond a glass half filled with brown liquid from a bottle. It was labelled Glenmorangie. Esmond looked at the date on the front of the bottle. It was a very tattered label and said the contents were twenty years old.

'Are you sure this is all right?' he asked doubtfully. 'Isn't it long past its sell-by date?'

'Past its sell-by date? Didn't your dad ever teach you anything about whisky?' Albert gurgled. 'I mean, he drank enough of the stuff.'

'Too much. That's why he's ill now.'

Albert kept his opinion of the real cause of Horace Wiley's illness to himself. Looking at Belinda making eyes at this gormless youth, he was beginning to understand his brother-in-law, and why a man who had previously been a relatively modest drinker had almost overnight taken to drinking to huge excess. More astonishingly still, he'd planned to kill, dismember and dissolve the bits and pieces of his son in nitric acid – which, gormless or not, seemed a bit harsh.

As Esmond sipped the whisky and said that, actually, he didn't terribly like the taste after all, Albert had a sudden insight: the stupid fellow was exactly the same as his father, or at least as his father had been as a young man. Albert had never understood why Vera had married such a staid and boring fellow. He'd told her she was completely daft at the time but then he'd never understood her either. As a teenager she was forever reading sloppy novels and Albert had never had any interest in books. The only ones that held his attention were those that contained debit and credit columns.

Albert had left school as early as he could and, with that criminal ruthlessness that had so horrified Horace, had quickly made himself what he called 'a tidy sum'. Exactly how much amounted to a 'tidy sum' was a closely kept secret which many would have been very keen to find out. The official version made for a modest claim but sufficient to satisfy the income tax men and to shut up those from Customs & Excise, although they continued to waste time trying to pin evasion on him. Even his accountant, chosen because he was renowned for his scrupulous honesty and integrity, had no idea what his client's true income was – or how he managed to enjoy such a lavish lifestyle on the modest income he declared.

When quizzed about his standard of living, Albert shamelessly confessed that he'd married for money and, oddly enough, there was more than a modicum of truth in the statement. Although, on closer inspection, Belinda's ongoing income appeared to be nil, and what money she had in her private bank account had in reality been transferred from Albert's.

It was all most peculiar. But none of that mattered now. What currently occupied Albert's devious mind was finding some way to use this young dummy, with his bank-manager-in-training looks and attire, to his advantage. He certainly wasn't having him hanging round the house with Belinda in her present mood. She'd been behaving quite oddly lately – he'd half wondered if it could be the menopause, though knew she was far too young for that.

No, if they were going to be stuck with the lad for

some time, which it looked as though they were, he would put him to use somewhere in the business. But first he would see exactly what this nephew of his was made of, and teaching him a little about the pleasures of alcohol seemed an excellent place to start.

Chapter 15

In the kitchen, Belinda's thoughts had nothing to do with toy boys. She was wondering why she had ever left home for this bungalow in Essexford where the country was so flat and life unutterably dull, where all that seemed to matter was money and all Albert's friends were crooks.

Belinda had had bouts of homesickness before but had overcome them by telling herself over and over again that she had everything a modern housewife could ever wish for and that she was secure for life. She had acted her part perfectly, but recently she had begun to see that it was no more than that: an act in a dull and in many ways tawdry, not to say sordid, play which had nothing to do with the person she really was. Unlike her awful sister-in-law, Vera Wiley, whose self, in so far as she had one, was a fantasy derived from her ghastly reading combined with sickening sentimentality and rank stupidity.

What's more, Belinda realised she had no authority in her marriage – a marriage which she now thoroughly regretted – and a loss of power she bitterly regretted too. But she preserved the ghastly decor she only pretended to like, made Albert take his shoes off when he came into their showcase of a house and generally acted the part of an autocrat. In fact, the trappings of the marriage – the modern furniture and the barely used but hugely expensive gadgets – were her only means of retaining some slight degree of self-respect and at the same time disguising her true feelings from Albert. At heart she longed to get away from the place and from his dreadful friends and to return to her true home, the house where she had grown up and where she was truly loved and respected.

Belinda finished making the supper and went through to the sitting room. If anything were to confirm the dark thoughts she had been brooding on in the kitchen, it was the scene that greeted – a wholly inappropriate word – her: Esmond Wiley lay, quite literally, before her. Having been plied with half a dozen different varieties of whisky and a couple of lethal brandies for good measure by his uncle, he had vomited, first down the front of his shirt and tie and then, onto the carpet. Albert, who had also been hitting the bottle in anticipation of the scene his wife was bound to make when she entered, was slumped in his armchair giggling insanely at the havoc he had brought.

'Couldn't hold his liquor,' said Albert, with a slur. 'Teaching him the diff . . . the difference bet . . . between good malt whisky and your blended muck an . . . French . . . Frog brandy. An' he couldn't take it. He couldn't take it.'

He giggled again and reached for the bottle on the floor beside his chair. But Belinda was there before him, and in any case it was empty.

'You bloody fool,' she snapped before reaching to feel for Esmond's pulse. It didn't seem to be beating at all strongly. She straightened up and shook Albert who seemed to have fallen asleep. 'You really are a bloody moron. I'm going to send for an ambulance.'

Albert woke and goggled drunkenly at her.

'Wha' for? I don' need a fuckin' ambu . . . amblance,' he managed to slur out.

Belinda looked at him with loathing. Albert was a lot drunker than she'd seen him for a very long time.

'You've gone too far this time. Getting the poor boy dead drunk, and I do mean dead, or will be soon.' She paused to let this sink in. 'He needs medical attention – and fast. If you don't believe me go and feel his pulse.'

Albert managed to get up but promptly fell back down on his knees – in Esmond's vomit. He cursed and grabbed Esmond's arm.

'I can't find his pulse,' he whimpered. 'He hasn't got one.'

For a moment, Belinda thought about pointing out that, of course, if Albert looked for it above his nephew's elbow, he hadn't, but she changed her mind. If she let the drunken swine believe he had killed Esmond, she would have him at her mercy. The thought of what Vera would do when she learnt that Albert had murdered her only son by forcing the lad to drink an enormous number of neat whiskies and brandies would put the fear of God Almighty up him.

'That's what I told you. I said you'd drunk him to death. Now what are you going to do? Vera will skin you alive. And slowly.'

Albert groaned, and was sick himself. He shared Belinda's opinion of Vera's reaction. It didn't bear trying to think about.

Meanwhile, Belinda was thinking. She had had an extraordinary idea. It was the culmination of her silent soliloquy in the kitchen.

'You'll just have to drive him to the hospital,' she said, laying the bait. 'You can tell them you found him by the roadside. That way his mother won't know you killed him.'

Albert stared glassily up at her. 'I didn't kill him. He drank himself to death. He's just like his bloody father. And I'm not driving anyone anywhere,' he managed to slur out with difficulty. 'I can't barely get up, let alone drive. I'm miles over the limit.

You wouldn't want me to lose my licence, would you? You'll have to take him. Go on, Belinda love, do it for me.'

Belinda smiled. He'd swallowed the bait hook, line and sinker. The idiot was going to lose a lot more than his licence by the time the night was over. Leaving Albert lying on the carpet, amid the regurgitated contents of both his and Esmond's stomachs, she dragged her nephew through the kitchen to the garage and to Albert's most precious car, the Aston Martin. After a short rest to draw breath, she heaved Vera Wiley's most treasured possession into the front seat, adjusted the safety belt and pulled up the convertible's hood.

For a moment Belinda hesitated. Was there anything she needed to take with her? No, she had everything she needed, she decided – except money.

She went back into the house and gently opened the door to the sitting room, glancing briefly at where Albert lay snoring on the floor, before shutting and locking it. Moving through to the bedroom, she dragged up a corner of the thick Dralon carpet and lifted the wooden board that covered the safe. A moment later, she had punched in the numbers on the keypad and removed the fifty thousand pounds in used notes hidden there by Albert. Finally, she reset the electronic lock to a different code so that he'd find it impossible to open the safe.

Back in the kitchen, she put the kettle and a

saucepan of milk on the stove and fetched two thermoses. Into one she ladled several tablespoons of coffee, and the other, Horlicks and a small sleeping pill. The latter was for Esmond should he wake from his drunken slumber. It didn't seem likely but she was taking no chances.

By the time Belinda drove out of the garage there was nothing to indicate that she had left the bungalow – and indeed Essex – for good. Beside her, Esmond Wiley, now wrapped in a blanket, remained dead to the world. He would almost certainly sleep through the night and awake with a hangover to beat all hangovers in a place beyond his wildest imaginings.

So too would Albert. She'd put an open bottle of Chivas Regal on the floor beside him, knowing he'd almost certainly take a swig from it as a pick-me-up when he came round. She liked to think what he'd feel like in the morning. Too awful for words.

Chapter 16

In his hotel room, Horace was tipsy and happy. He'd celebrated successfully booking his passage with a first-rate dinner and more than one bottle of champagne. He was now lying on his bed trying to make up his mind where to go to after Latvia. He was reasonably confident that his roundabout route and various subterfuges would make tracing him unlikely, but knowing how determined Vera could be when she set her mind to something, taking in a couple more countries after Latvia was going to be vital.

Horace needed to go to places where no one would think of looking for him. He'd already considered Finland only to dismiss it as too cold. Norway and Sweden were out too. As was Spain. What he'd seen of Benidorm on the box had put him off Spain for good and the Costa del Sol was rightly, in his opinion, known as the Costa del Crime because so many British crooks had villas there. Nor did France hold any attraction for him. It was too close to Britain for one thing, and for another, he was of a generation that had been brought up to dislike the French and to believe that extramarital sex was the main spare-time occupation of the entire population of that much-maligned country. Horace had had enough predatory sex imposed on him by Vera to last him a lifetime.

In fact, no country in Europe attracted him. He needed somewhere entirely different from the England he knew and the life he had been forced to live since his marriage. Finally, unable to make a decision, he finished the champagne and fell asleep.

Chapter 17

Vera Wiley remained miserably awake. She had lost her love child to the Ponsons and, with unusual insight, she realised that they were bound to lead him into bad ways. It was all Horace's fault. For the first time in her life, Vera lost her faith in the fantasy world of the romantic trash she had marinated her mind in for so many years. The only thing she could hope for was that Horace would come to his senses so that Esmond would be able to return home as soon as possible. In the meantime she would keep Horace on short rations and let him suffer. She hadn't bothered to give him supper and she had half a mind to let him go without his breakfast too. He was going to learn not to drink himself into a nervous break-down, and if he didn't like it, he could divorce her. She wouldn't care. She no longer had any illusions about him.

Chapter 18

Belinda Ponson had no sooner left the garage in the Aston Martin than she realised she had made a mistake in taking the car. It was far too conspicuous for her journey. So she drove to Albert's second-hand car lot, grabbed the keys to a Ford from the office cupboard and, after a bit of a struggle, managed to transfer the still-comatose Esmond to the back seat. There were several similar cars in the lot and it was unlikely to be missed immediately. To confuse the situation still further, she then drove the Aston Martin to the hospital car park where she abandoned it, before walking back to the car lot.

Esmond still lolled as she had left him. The time was ten forty-five and she had a long drive ahead of her. As she drove, she laid her plans. She would stick to side roads to avoid the CCTV cameras on the motorway, and go across country rather than direct. This would make the journey much longer, but it was worth it. Nobody, particularly Albert, must know where she'd gone. And so she drove through the night without tiring and kept well within the speed limit.

It was just as the eastern sky was beginning to lighten and full dawn was soon to break that the old Ford breasted a long steep hill. Belinda cut the engine and sat still until it was possible to see the landscape far below. Its bleakness was entirely as she remembered it from her childhood holidays. She had been happy then and that sense of happiness now flooded back to her. Nothing had changed. In the distance she could make out the looming shape of Grope Hall. In her own way she was coming home.

Chapter 19

Far to the south, Albert spent the night in part on the unsavoury carpet and later, when he discovered he couldn't open the sitting-room door and that the keys to the house had mysteriously disappeared from his pocket, thrashing around on the Dralon sofa, periodically taking slugs from the Chivas Regal he'd found lying by his side. At 4 a.m. he was desperate to reach his own bed and even more desperate to relieve himself.

'Belinda,' he bawled drunkenly and repeatedly. 'Belinda, you bitch, let me out.'

In the end, unable to open the triple-glazed, bullet-proofed windows, he rather inaccurately hurled two empty whisky bottles at them, cursed Belinda a great many times and, as the last straw, cut his hand rather badly searching for some more substantial Scotch bottles in the drinks cabinet. Finally, realising he was in need of some medical self-help if he didn't want to bleed to death, he used his handkerchief to bandage his hand as best he could.

Albert was still suffering from a painful head and hand when the front doorbell chimed, although he had alleviated his other agony by peeing in the giant fern Belinda had been cultivating in the corner of the sitting room. He staggered to his feet and went to open it before remembering that he was locked in, and that the keys were missing. He peered at the CCTV screen used to check visitors but it was dead and refused to work. All the same, he could hear Vera screaming, 'Let me in, let me in.'

Albert should have guessed she would come to check if her bloody adolescent love child was safe and well. Considering his own hangover he was damned certain Esmond's was infinitely worse. Best not to try to open the door. Vera wouldn't stand there all day. She'd go and telephone and he wouldn't answer. Half an hour later she did and he didn't. He was too busy trying to kick the sitting-room door down.

Vera concluded that her brother and darling son must be working at the Ponson second-hand car showroom, and set off on foot in that direction. But it was Sunday and the garage was shut. Foiled there she trudged back to the bungalow, prowled round to the rear and tried the back door and attempted to peer through its black-glazed windows. That didn't help. Nor did hammering on the kitchen windows since it only provoked a volley of shots, some of which pinged alarmingly against the triple-glazed armoured glass. Vera slid down the wall under the window in a state of panic. She redoubled her screams without getting any response apart from the sound of even more shots.

For the first time, she had to hand it to Horace. He'd said her brother was a gangster and one day he'd get his comeuppance. By the sound of things that day had come. Not that she really cared what happened to Albert. It was the presence of her darling Esmond in what sounded like the Gunfight at the OK Corral that sent her into hysterics: little did she know that she need not have worried.

Inside the bungalow, Albert Ponson had finally thought of a way of getting through to the kitchen and had emptied his Colt .45 automatic into the lock. Gaining entry only to find the back door also locked incensed him, so much so that he began firing indiscriminately, the bullets ricocheting off expensive appliances, puncturing several stainless-steel saucepans in a cupboard and the Kenwood mixer in the process.

At the sound of this new burst of gunfire Vera finally took action. Something terrible was happening in the bungalow and her darling Esmond was in there. She dashed into the street and used her mobile phone to call the police station.

'There's shooting going on in my brother's house,' she screamed.

The police seemed only vaguely interested. 'Really? And who's your brother?'

'Albert Ponson. They're murdering him.'

'And what's your name?'

'I'm Mrs Wiley and Albert's my brother.'

At the police station the news was greeted calmly. A voice in the background seemed to be saying it was about time the bugger bought it.

'Address?'

'Which one?' demanded Vera, now thoroughly confused.

'Yours of course. We know where Al Ponson's garage is.'

But Vera had reached the end of her tether.

'I told you, the shooting's up at his house – Ponson Place – not mine. For God's sake hurry. My darling son's in there with him.'

'Your what?'

'My darling son Esmond. I left him with Albert yesterday to protect him and now there's all this shooting and – '

But the inspector didn't want to hear any more. He covered the receiver with his hand and handed it to a sergeant. 'We've got a right nutter up there bleating on about her darling son Esmond and how she's given him to our local Al Capone for protection.'

120

The sergeant listened for a moment and put the phone down hurriedly.

'Some hysterical woman says there's shooting up at Ponson Place,' he told the constable. 'Pray to God she's right. So move. It will give us a chance to see what that bastard's got in his fortified house at any rate.'

Five minutes later, with Vera wailing behind them, the inspector, the sergeant and the constable (backed up by two further policemen on the grounds that you never knew what you might find when you crossed paths with the Ponsons) were hammering on the front door and ordering Albert to open up.

He would happily have done so if he could have got the lock to work, but not only was the back-door key missing, thanks to Belinda cutting the entire electrical system off, the whole place was also in total darkness.

For the first time Albert cursed the metal plates he had installed over the windows and doors to the outside to prevent burglars and nosy neighbours seeing the orgies he called parties. He used his remaining bullets to fire his way from the kitchen through into the garage only to find the electronic doors firmly down and with no chance of raising them. Not only that, his Aston Martin wasn't there. The car was known to be his pride and joy which he treasured more than anything else. That suggested to Albert that an organised crime syndicate was responsible and that he could be looking at either kidnapping or, worse still, murder.

With his head throbbing he tried to think. If Belinda and Esmond had been kidnapped or murdered, the intrusion of the law was the last thing he needed. Peering through the keyhole in the door, he was only slightly relieved to see his damned sister being forced into an ambulance by five hefty policemen.

Ten minutes later, the chief inspector had joined his five colleagues outside the Ponson bungalow. He was taking his turn in trying to persuade Albert to come out only to be repeatedly told that he was a complete arse. Didn't he understand that Albert couldn't because the electronic lock wouldn't work. And that even if the arsing lock would work, the arsing keys were missing.

The chief inspector tried being reasonable. 'No one's accusing you of anything. We just want to know what the trouble is.'

'The fucking trouble is that I'm locked in my bloody house and I can't get out, you stupid dick. How many times do I have to tell you?' Albert shouted back. 'And some swine's stolen my Aston Martin into the bargain.'

The chief inspector tried another tack.

'Have there been any shots in the house?'

'Have there been any what?' screamed Albert, still hung-over and now thoroughly muddled. Befuddled was the better word.

'Has anyone been shooting in the house?'

Albert struggled to think.

'Yes,' he said finally. 'I shot the lock off the sitting-room door.'

'I see,' said the chief inspector, who didn't. He continued after a long pause. 'And why do that?'

'Because some bugger didn't want me to get out.'

'Who wouldn't?'

'Whoever locked the bloody thing.'

'What bloody thing was behind the door?' he asked, perked up by the supposition that it was a person.

'I don't know. It was pitch dark like I told you.'

'So you fired through the lock and hit someone on the other side.'

'No I didn't. When I looked in the kitchen I didn't see anyone. How could I? It was pitch dark. I told you that.'

'So how come you said someone was bloody?'

Distracted by a large lorry hooting at a tractor in its path, the sergeant lost track of the statement he was taking down and concentrated on that 'bloody'. The 'whoever' didn't help.

'So you admit you shot the person who had locked you out of the kitchen?' he said.

Albert struggled vainly to think of an innocent answer. 'I didn't know there was anyone on the other side. I couldn't even see the lock. Had to feel for it. I mean, I put my finger out until I found the lock and then put the muzzle up against it and pulled the trigger. I didn't mean to shoot anyone.'

The chief inspector took over from the sergeant.

'How do you know your Aston Martin has been stolen?'

'Because it's not in the garage.'

'Is the door between the kitchen and the garage locked too?'

'Not now it isn't.'

'And you say it has been stolen? How do you know?'

'Because the car isn't there. I felt all over the place and it's missing.'

'Well, if there's access from the garage to the kitchen, the only thing is to bring up a bulldozer and drag that garage door down.'

Albert Ponson stood horrified in the darkness.

'You can't do that,' he squawked. 'You'll bring the whole front of the house down.'

'We're only going to push it open. May damage the door of course but – '

'You don't understand. You push it or drag it and the whole front is going to come down, all of it.'

'All of the front wall of the house? Of course it won't. You just don't want us to come in. You've got something to hide in there.'

'Like what?'

'Like a dead body. Like this nephew your sister keeps banging on about.'

'You're out of your fucking mind,' shrieked Albert. 'I haven't touched him.'

'Then why isn't he saying anything? If he's in there

with you, let him say something – provided he's still alive, that is.'

'Oh God, oh God, I'm going mad,' Albert moaned.

'Is that what you're going to plead in court? That you're out of your mind, that you're a homicidal maniac? And where is Mrs Ponson? Is she dead too?'

Albert slumped to the floor and whimpered, in the darkness inadvertently seating himself in a pool of oil. Outside, the chief inspector and the inspector smiled happily and crossed the road.

'I reckon we've finally got the bastard,' the chief inspector said gleefully. 'I've been waiting years for this day. He'll get life plus, as sure as eggs is eggs.'

'Why do you think the place is in darkness?' said the inspector. 'It doesn't make sense.'

'The old bird we sent down to the hospital was right after all. She did hear shots. That would have been when he killed the lad. Then, having got the body out of the house, and probably having dumped it somewhere, he comes back and puts a bullet through the main electricity cable so he's got some sort of alibi. There must have been blood on the carpet or wher-ever and he'd have got rid of that far away from the body. In a river or somewhere like that.'

'And the car? What's he done with that?'

'Same as the carpet, or perhaps flogged it,' the chief inspector said. 'There's almost certainly blood on it too.'

They were interrupted by a tracked bulldozer that

was grinding up the road. The two police officers crossed the road towards the garage.

'Put the hook over the top,' the chief inspector ordered.

There was a scream from inside the garage.

'For shit's sake, don't pull the fucking thing, I've told you the whole front will come down. I mean the house.'

'I can't see how. I mean, we're only going to drag that gate down. Shove the bloody great hook over the top and stand clear, lads.'

As the bulldozer moved up, and the huge hook at the end of the chain was pushed over the top of the metal gate, Albert shouted even more frantically.

'The gate's let into the wall of the house, for Christ's sake.'

'Pull the other one, Al, you crook,' the sergeant shouted back. 'You've got something hidden inside.'

The bulldozer had gone into reverse and as the chain took up the strain, it was clear that Albert Ponson had been telling the truth. The entire front of the house was moving forward. Seconds later, the roof tilted and then, as the wall fell into the garden, the roof dropped after it.

When the wall started to shift, Albert had had the sense to race to the back of the bungalow and was now lying under a bed close to a column on top of which two steel girders rested that had previously supported the roof. Above him, the darkened sky began to indicate rain. When the roof's fall forwards had finally stopped, he crawled out, shocked by the noise, the cement and the concrete dust, and above all by the demise of his dream house. To add to the horror of the situation, several water pipes had broken in the bathrooms and one perverse pipe directly above his head was taking excellent aim at his face. As Albert opened his mouth to scream for help, while trying to disentangle his left leg from some electric cables, he realised he was in acute danger of drowning. Then came the thought that one of those bloody coppers might take it into his head to switch the electricity on in which case he'd be electrocuted as well.

With a desperate, not to say frantic, effort, Albert pulled his leg free and used it to kick the wires away. Heaving himself out of the now shattered window frame, he crawled through the undergrowth and went to hide in the depths of a large evergreen shrub. Lying there, trying to steady his still-shaking limbs, he suddenly remembered the small fortune locked in the safe under the carpet in the bedroom.

Screw it. He wasn't going to crawl back and get it now while the police were around. He'd have to wait until they'd made themselves scarce.

As it was, he could hear that bloody bulldozer, evidently still with the gate attached by the hook and chain to a large section of the front wall since it seemed to be trying to get rid of these encumbrances and, by the sound of scraping metal, not succeeding.

Exhausted and stunned at the destruction of his home, Albert Ponson passed out.

Chapter 20

In front of what had been the bungalow, the police had been joined by the superintendent who was considering the consequences to his career of what could only be called a total catastrophe.

'You bloody moron,' he shouted at the chief inspector. 'I asked you to arrest this Ponson crook, not knock his blasted house to the ground. You've almost certainly killed the bastard. You wouldn't have made a competent parking attendant let alone a kindergarten crossing keeper. The front-page headlines of every paper in the country are going to blazon this little lot out. POLICE TERRORISTS BLOW HOUSE UP and WHO NEEDS TERRORISTS WHEN WE'VE GOT THE SECURITY POLICE? As sure as hell I'll lose my job. Well, let me tell you this: when I go, you're going a fucking sight further down.'

'But how were we to know he'd got an armour-plated bungalow? The old bird, his sister, said her son was in there to protect the lad from his father and that she'd heard gunshots. We had to get in.'

The superintendent looked insanely round.

'Are you telling me she was married to her brother? That's incest, that is.'

'No, she's married to a bank manager in Croydon who's gone off his rocker and tried to kill his son with a carving knife. She said we had to get him out of his uncle's house.'

'What? Before he killed him too?' asked the superintendent.

'That's right, sir.'

'Instead of which he left you to do it for him by bringing the place down. And where is this Mrs Ponson now?'

'Well, inside too, I suppose.'

'You mean she heard gunshots and her son being killed and – '

'No, sir. Her name is Mrs Wiley. She's down at Accident and Emergency.'

'Reverse that order of words, Chief Inspector. Emergency and Accident. In fact, cut out the Accident altogether. This was deliberate and you're responsible. Wait till we've an inquest and after that the trial and see what the verdict is.'

130

He turned and was about to get as far away as quickly as possible when the chief inspector stopped him.

'Hadn't you better question Mrs Wiley first, sir?'

The superintendent turned and tried vainly to remember who Mrs Wiley was. He was feeling even madder now.

'Is she still alive? I thought you said her husband tried to kill her with a carving knife.'

'Not her. Her son. Mr Wiley is a bank manager. He took a carving knife and – '

'Oh yes, I remember now. She brought him up to this wrecked bungalow to have him shot by the bigamist husband she'd married before the bank manager. All right, we'll go and see her. I don't believe I've ever met a bigamist before.'

The chief inspector kept his mouth shut. He was wondering if the superintendent had been drinking, and he was wishing he could have a stiff whisky himself.

Chapter 21

Waking in London following yet another self-indulgent evening, Horace wasn't feeling too well, not least because he'd woken to discover that he'd overslept and the tramp steamer had long since left on its voyage.

After a minimal lunch he finally felt able to leave the hotel and, realising that buying another ticket at the same travel agency might make even the dozy clerk there suspicious, he took a taxi to the most lawless part of London, near Docklands.

Deciding that he needed to better cover his tracks, he chose the nastiest second-hand clothing shop he could find and bought a shabby raincoat and a pair of thoroughly disreputable boots several sizes too big for him. Using the cover of a public lavatory to change, he stuffed the bottom of some old and grubby trousers he'd had the foresight to bring from his gardener's shed into them. By the time he emerged Horace was even more unrecognisable as a fugitive bank manager.

He then made his way by bus to Docklands itself. After a tortuous journey the bus stopped and, cursing his aching head, Horace walked up and down until he found a shipping office, where he paid – with considerable difficulty – for another ticket to Latvia.

'Going back to your own country, are you?' asked the clerk, who looked like an immigrant himself, when he'd read the printed request Horace presented him asking him for a boat ticket for Riga. 'Can't say I blame you.'

Horace nodded, and clutching the ticket and his suitcase, went in search of another public lavatory to change back into his suit.

Back at the hotel he wrote to his Swiss bank and told the manager he'd always dealt with that he wanted to withdraw three hundred thousand pounds in cash – he had a business deal in Australia, the story went, and would be over personally to collect it before the end of the month. That still left him with well over a million pounds on deposit.

The next morning, dressed once again in his grubby clothes – which earned him a very funny look at the front desk – he paid his hotel bill, picked up his suitcase and left, tipping the porter very handsomely as he went. The porter, obviously thinking Horace needed the money more than he did, not only returned the tip but doubled it.

Not quite satisfied that he'd be impossible to follow, Horace spent the next night sleeping rough on Blackheath, an experience he determined never to repeat after being twice moved on by the local police force and once taken for a urinal by a local tramp.

By mid-morning the following day he was back at the shipping office, where he tipped the clerk one hundred pounds and flashed his passport very briefly in front of him. Not that it was necessary. The man was so pleased to have been so well tipped that he let Horace through without bothering to note his name down. Delighted at his tactics, Mr Ludwig Jansens went up the gangway determined never to set foot in England again.

Chapter 22

At Grope Hall, Belinda had opened the gate and driven the Ford down to the house, ignoring the two bulls by the side of the track and the sound of the barking dogs round the back. Driving right up to the kitchen door, she got out and knocked. A very old woman peered out of a bedroom window.

'What do you want?' she demanded.

'I'm your niece, Belinda. My mother was Eudora, your sister. Eliza was my grandmother.'

'Eudora? Eudora?' called the old woman, clearly puzzled. 'Where's your mother, Eudora?'

'No, I'm Belinda. Eudora's dead. She died two years ago. She had pneumonia. I thought you knew. I wrote to you at the time.'

'I don't read letters. Can't because my glasses don't work. And don't want to anyway. Always bad news.' The old woman paused and appeared to be thinking. 'Why have you come here? If you are Eudora's daughter, as you say you are, she surely told you how the family has always lived.'

'Oh, yes, she did. At least the most important facts. The head of the family must be a woman. When Eliza died you succeeded her. We used to come and visit when I was little, don't you remember?'

'My mind's not what it was. Not that it was ever much in the first place. I remember Eudora going down south to look for a man but I don't know anything since then. How do I know you are who you say you are?'

'I'm a Grope to the core and I can prove it if you let me.'

The old woman nodded, and then asked, 'When was your mother's birthday?'

'Twentieth of June. She was born in 1940.'

'That's true. Well, you'd better come in. The door is unlocked. I'm not up and dressed yet but I'll be down in a while and you can tell me why you've come here.'

Belinda checked to make sure that Esmond was still asleep before letting herself into the house. She went through the scullery and stood looking at the kitchen. It was just as she remembered it as a child. The same deal table in the middle and the same pots and pans on the shelves or hanging from hooks on the wall opposite the ancient coal stove. Everything was as it had been when she'd seen the place on her last visit with her mother all those years before. Even the smell of bacon was the same, and . . . She couldn't identify them individually. They were simply the mingled smells she had known over a period of six years as a child. Best of all, they had none of the qualities that she had escaped from in her kitchen at Ponson Place. Nothing shone or gleamed white like her washing machine and the various gadgets she had amassed over the years. At the time she had found some comfort in that awful modern kitchen. Or forced herself to believe she had. But now she had really come to her proper home where she had spent the happiest times of her childhood.

Oddly enough, in spite of the hours and hours she had driven along country roads, always keeping within the speed limit to avoid the police cameras, she had no feeling of fatigue. The dawn breaking over the hills, the vast fields and distant woods had given her fresh energy. And arriving here at Grope Hall and seeing that nothing had changed was the biggest boost of all.

Belinda returned to the car where Esmond was still out for the count on the back seat under the blanket. She would need help to get him into the house. Back in the kitchen she made some coffee and waited for someone to arrive who might help carry Esmond to a bedroom. Strangely, now that she was here, nothing seemed very urgent any more.

Presently she saw a middle-aged man come out of a barn with a bucket, and called him over. He obviously worked on the Grope estate.

'What's your name?' she asked.

'They call me Old Samuel.'

'Old Samuel? You're not that old, Samuel.'

'No, but there's always been an Old Samuel in the Grope household, so when the previous Old Samuel died and I came here, that was when I was twenty-seven like, I got called Old. My name's not Samuel either — it's Jeremy — but old Mrs Grope wouldn't stand for it and Old Samuel I became and Old Samuel I stay. I run the farm and do odd jobs around the place now that there's only the old lady left.'

'I wonder if you would help me get someone out of my car? He's sleeping off too much alcohol.'

They crossed to the Ford.

'I should say he is,' said Old Samuel when he opened the rear door and breathed in the fumes from the back of the car. He reached in and pulled Esmond out from under the blanket.

'It will take him a good few days to work whatever he's drunk off. That it will. Smells to me like whisky. Where do you want him put?'

'In the bedroom over the kitchen.'

Old Samuel looked at her with interest. She obviously knew the Hall very well. In fact, by the look of her, and the fact that she had an unconscious young bloke in the back of her car, she might well be a Grope herself. She was certainly looking pretty happy with life.

Chapter 23

The same could not be said of Esmond. He'd slept on for hours in an alcoholic haze and after being moved to the bedroom above the kitchen had only struggled out of bed to have a pee. The trouble was that the room had no bathroom, and the only pisspot was against the wall under the bed. In trying to reach it he'd fallen out of bed and couldn't get back in. So instead he'd pulled the blankets off the bed and simply wet the carpet before falling asleep once again.

Belinda had drawn the dark curtains across when Samuel had brought Esmond upstairs with her help and locked the bedroom door before she had gone to bed herself, finally exhausted by her long slow drive in the old Ford. She woke late in the afternoon and went through to check on Esmond. He was sitting on the side of the bed gazing down at the wet patch on the floor and looking awful.

'What you need is a good meal.'

'Where am I, Auntie Belinda?' he asked, staring out the window at the fells rolling away to the horizon.

'You've come home. This is where you belong.'

'Home? This isn't my home. Home's in South Croydon.'

'And I'm not your auntie, I'm your fiancée. We're going to get married, remember?'

'Married? We can't. You're married already and you're my aunt. You're Mrs Ponson, the wife of that horrible crook, Uncle Albert.'

'Oh my poor boy. You've been ill for a very long time, dear. We were married but we got a divorce. Don't you remember, you made me run away with you?' Belinda hesitated for a moment. 'And another thing, you must never use the name Ponson. I insist on that. Your family name is Grope, same as mine, and your Christian name is Joe. When anyone asks you, you're to say you are Joe Grope. Say it.'

'Joe Grope.'

'And you come from Lyle Road, Ealing. Have you got that?'

Esmond nodded. 'I'm Joe Grope from Lyle Road, Ealing. Where's that?'

'In London. Now you're to repeat your new name over and over again. Do you understand?'

144

'Yes. I'm Joe Grope from Ealing. But why do I have to be Joe Grope from Ealing?'

'Never mind that right now. Come along with me and you can have a nice big breakfast. You obviously need one.'

They went downstairs to the kitchen and while Esmond sat at the scrubbed and ancient deal table, Belinda fried eggs and bacon and made strong coffee. The bewildered Esmond repeated his new name again and again. By the end of the meal he was feeling better, a bit better but not well enough to notice Belinda slip a small tablet into his coffee.

By the time Esmond had drunk it he was drifting off to sleep again and Belinda had to help him up to the bedroom where she remade the bed and pulled the chamber pot out so he could reach it easily. After that she undressed him and put him to bed. By that time he was really deeply asleep and the sleeping pill in his coffee ensured he wouldn't wake until the following morning.

Downstairs, Belinda explained her plan to her aunt who had waited long enough to find out why her niece had turned up and with a strange young lad in tow. Belinda let a few tears escape as she described her miserable marriage and her dreadful sister-in-law.

'I've left that awful man and his horrid modern bungalow,' she sobbed. 'You have no idea how beastly it was down there. And for years he drank himself stupid. With any luck it will kill him. And he insisted on having stupid parties and going off to get thieves to steal cars. Oh, he paid them well enough. Worst of all he was sterile and he'd never have produced daughters anyway. All he was interested in was money. Well, I've put paid to that. I brought with me every penny he'd hidden under the floor in my room to help you out.'

'You didn't kill him, did you, Belinda?' Myrtle asked, curious rather than shocked.

'No, I didn't. Though maybe I should have.'

'But who is that boy you've bought with you and why does he keep calling himself Esmond?'

'I've changed the boy's name. He's now Joe Grope and if anyone asks, not that they will up here, he comes from Ealing in west London, not Croydon.'

'But why did you bring him at all?'

'Because I wanted to rescue him. His mother is Albert's sister and just as dreadful in a different way. She's as sentimental as a sponge soaked in treacle. Calls her son "darling" every time she speaks about him. That or "my little love child", and he's six foot tall. It's utterly sickening.'

'What's his father say?'

'Tried to kill the boy with a knife. That's why his awful mother brought him up to our place for protection. Of course Albert had to agree. She's as formidable as he is, in a different kind of way. Don't ask me why. Anyway, my wretched husband got him blind drunk and passed out himself. That's when I decided to bring him up to Grope Hall. He's at least going to remain sober here and I thought that he could make himself useful on the farm.'

'There is that,' said her aunt. 'Men my age have been difficult to come by since the War. I suppose they got themselves killed and since my Harold died, I haven't the energy or the looks to go and find another one. Besides, I couldn't give birth to anything at my age and we need a girl into the bargain.'

'That's what I thought, which is another reason I brought him here. We're going to get married and have children and he can work on the farm. Nobody's going to find us now that I've changed his name and I'm sick and tired of being a virtual virgin. I could be a human vibrator for that masturbating Albert, and if he doesn't masturbate, I don't want to catch Aids or syphilis from the sluts he sleeps with, which I'm certain he does. I want a really active young fellow who's healthy.'

'Where is he now?' Myrtle asked.

'Sleeping off all that filthy alcohol Albert filled him up with yesterday.'

'And this Albert is your former husband? Are you sure he doesn't know where you've gone?'

'Absolutely. You don't think I ever told him I'm a Grope? I'm not as daft as all that. In any case my mother, my late mother that is, didn't give her name as Grope on the marriage certificate. She said she was a Miss Lyle and produced her best friend's birth certificate.'

Belinda paused for breath and briefly wondered how Albert bloody Ponson was getting on before picking up where she left off in describing how she'd finally come home.

Chapter 24

Had Albert been able to read Belinda's mind he'd have replied that she was insane to suppose he was getting on at all. He'd spent the past few hours blaming his brother-in-law for having a nervous breakdown in the first place (even though he now understood why Horace had tried to kill his idiot son), cursing his sister for dumping the wretched boy on him, wondering whether Belinda really had been kidnapped and, of course, freezing. It might be summer but being a British one it had rained and Albert had been unable to find anywhere more waterproof than the shrub under which he had originally hidden. He was prevented from seeking shelter in his wrecked bungalow by the presence of a police inspector in a raincoat who was guarding the back of the ruined bungalow. Inside, the discoveries made by the three detectives investigating the incident made things look even worse for the missing Albert. They had found blood on the carpet in the sitting room and some more in the kitchen. Finally, in the garage, where in searching for the Aston Martin Albert's makeshift bandage had come off, there was apparent proof that a terrible crime must have been committed. As Albert soaked in the garden the detectives stood in the relative warmth of the sitting room and discussed these findings together with the absence of Belinda Ponson and Esmond Wiley.

'No bloody wonder he didn't want the garage door pulled down. I'd say the murders had to have been done here. Of course he could have killed them in that fucking do-it-yourself slaughterhouse and dragged their bodies down here to the house and driven them off somewhere in his car that's gone missing,' one of them was heard to say.

'He'd have had to use something to carry each body in. He couldn't have got them down here any other way without leaving a massive trail of blood.'

'True enough,' said another, 'But what could he use? It would have to be water- and blood-proof.'

'You've obviously never been down to Ponson's slaughterhouse and seen what it's like. Go on. You can have my torch. Charlie's got a flashlight. Actually, I'd take that and check the plastic sheets and bags. You'll get a better impression.'

'All right, I will,' said the third detective and strode across the garden and the field confidently. He returned a different man.

'Dear God! I thought you were joking when you said it was a slaughterhouse. This swine Ponson is undoubtedly a murderer. What I don't understand is why there isn't any fresh blood down there. It's all dried out.'

The other two detective constables had to agree.

'I've never seen anything so horrible in my life. And to have a sign that it's a do-it-yourself slaughterhouse and then another that says "KILL & EAT YOUR OWN". The bastards.'

The other two kept quiet. They'd known Albert was the local crook and known that he encouraged farmers to slaughter their own beasts at a far cheaper cost than butchers charged. Not that that was a crime, nor that it mattered in the greater scheme of things. He'd always been a crook who if there was any justice ought to spend a good few years behind bars. But this was way over the top. The acres of encrusted blood at the slaughterhouse and the absence of his wife and the young fellow suggested that something truly appalling had happened to them.

Having scraped a sizeable amount of dried bloodstains off the bungalow floor and photographed the bloody handprints on the garage walls, they'd found an unused towel and mopped the fresh gore up with it. They searched the ruins again and added the spent

151

bullets and the vomit-stained rug to the evidence before returning to the police station.

Under the dripping shrub Albert caught snatches of the detectives' conversation and was horrified. He had built the DIY slaughterhouse to make enough money to fool the tax authorities and instead he had provided the police with awful suspicion. He hadn't foreseen the implications of the signage with its suggestion that he was a murdering cannibal. In fact, he had only recently removed an advert with the same invitation from the local paper when the vicar complained, but now that his wife and that stupid Esmond had disappeared the police would soon learn about it. Talk about the 'the fat being in the fire'.

To make matters worse still, the place was swilling with animal blood and if, as they were sure to do, they tried to detect human DNA samples, they would find it impossible to distinguish them from the gallons of pig and cattle gore that had accumulated over the years on the floor.

As Albert lay in the garden shivering with cold and wet he began to share the detective's belief that he'd spend a good few years behind bars, though for a crime he hadn't committed. Having come to this dire conclusion he waited until that damned policeman who'd been guarding the remains of the bungalow finally dozed off in a chair in the wreckage of the lounge. Once Albert was satisfied he was properly asleep, he crawled out of the shrubbery and tiptoed down the street towards the second-hand car lot. He'd get one of the less popular and conspicuous but fast and reliable cars and get the hell out of the area.

All the time he wondered where Belinda and Esmond were. Perhaps they were still at the hospital and Esmond was having his stomach washed out. In which case he'd better go down there himself . . .

On second and third thoughts, he didn't think this such a good idea. They might think he'd set out to get rid of the lout by way of alcohol poisoning and hold him on suspicion. Or they might take one look at the state he was in and simply call the police.

In the end, Albert decided it would be safer to stick with his first impulse and get the hell away from the area. He fetched the keys for a Honda and presently was driving at 100mph down towards Southend. Once he got there he would book into a bed and breakfast and not some smart hotel where they'd ask to carry his luggage and why he was so wet. No, he'd find somewhere cheap and modest where no questions would be asked. He'd pay cash too.

It was then that Albert remembered he had no cash on him and that his fortune was in the safe under the carpet in the bedroom. And just as he realised this, a police car with lights flashing forced him to brake and pull over to the side of the road.

An hour later he'd been breathalysed and was in police custody charged with driving over the alcohol and speed limits at 120mph in an unlicensed vehicle with faulty brakes and worn tyres.

'You'll come up before the district judge in the morning,' he was told, 'for dangerous driving and drunk too. Think yourself lucky. You could have killed yourself, and a lot of other people into the bargain.'

The officer was wrong. Next morning Albert was in a police van and being driven back to Essexford to be questioned by the superintendent who was now convinced that both Albert Ponson and his sister were psychopathic criminals.

Chapter 25

Vera Wiley, who had been sedated in A & E, had recovered completely by the time the superintendent arrived at the hospital. She sat up in bed and demanded her clothes. The superintendent told the doctor to move the bed into a private room and the doctor was only too happy to oblige. The other patients in the ward cheered. They were sick to death of Mrs Wiley screaming she wanted her darling love child Esmond back.

'Who is Esmond? Is he your husband?' asked the superintendent who had just been rung up by the Home Secretary's top assistant calling to tell him that the job of the police of whatever rank was to arrest criminals and not to destroy houses. He rang off before the superintendent could answer.

'He told me, "You can leave that to al-Qaeda,"' the superintendent told Vera.

'You mean my brother. He's not called Kyder. His name is Albert Ponson. Where's he got to? I left Esmond with him and he's supposed to be protecting him from my husband who tried to murder him.'

'What a pity he didn't succeed,' murmured the superintendent, thoroughly sick of the lot of them, and then immediately regretted it. Vera leapt out of bed and hurled her full weight on him. As his chair fell back onto the floor he landed on his back and slashed his head on the edge of the bedside cupboard. A doctor and two nurses carried him on a stretcher to have ten stitches in Accident and Emergency.

The chief inspector took over when several policemen had managed to force Vera back into bed and put handcuffs on her ankles.

'Try leaping out of bed with them on and you'll break your blasted legs,' she was told.

Vera lay back on the pillow weeping. 'I want to know what my brother Albert has done with Esmond. My husband tried to kill him. I've told you that before.'

'You mean he tried to kill Mr Ponson. Why did he want to do that?'

'Because he said there were three of him.'

'Three of him? Your husband has a twin brother? I mean, he has two twin brothers, like he's a triplet, is that what you're telling me? How do you know who's making love to you if that's the case?'

156

'I don't know what you're talking about,' screamed Vera.

'That makes two of us. Oh, of course, your husband tried to kill three bloody Ponsons. Well, I can't say I blame him. One Al is crooked enough.'

Vera stared at him dementedly.

'I didn't say that. You're putting words in my mouth,' Vera whimpered, wishing he could put some sensible ones in.

The chief inspector did his best to clear his mind and then started again.

'Just tell me who tried to kill two people. That's all I want to find out.'

'Horace did.'

'And Horace is your husband?'

'Of course he is. We've been married for twenty years.'

'OK. I've got that. So now he's gone down with some illness and you say he tried to kill Esmond. And Esmond is your only son?'

'Yes. He tried to stab him with the carving knife.'

The chief inspector came up with what he thought was a reasonable question.

'And was Esmond his real son? I mean, you hadn't been having it off with another man and got a bun in the oven from this other bloke?'

The expression was not one Vera knew.

'How could I have? I was cooking supper at the time.'

'I mean, had you been having a love affair with a man who wasn't your husband and got pregnant when he ejaculated?'

'When he what?' asked Vera, whose romantic reading had limited her vocabulary.

'When he came his load.'

'Load? What do you mean?'

'All right, let's just say making love.'

'But if we were he'd have had to be there. Not that we were.'

'Oh never mind. What I am trying to ascertain is why your husband tried to stab your son. That's all. He must have had a reason.'

'He said it was because Esmond was exactly like him.'

'I should have thought that would have reassured him you weren't having an affair with another man,' the chief inspector said.

'But I've told you, I'm not like that. I've always been completely faithful.'

The chief inspector could well believe it. Even a sex maniac wouldn't have been attracted to Mrs Wiley. Her husband must be utterly hideous himself. On this note he stopped the interview and went to see how the superintendent was getting on. He wasn't. The stitches hadn't taken and were having to be redone.

'It's bloody hell. Much more of this and I'll go off my rocker too.'

'Makes two of us. This is the weirdest case I've ever tried to understand.'

Chapter 26

Horace was not enjoying his voyage much either. A storm had blown up once they were away from England and the Thames and nowhere near Holland. In short, the tramp steamer was living up to its reputation and wallowing about in the North Sea in a way that certainly alarmed Horace Wiley. One moment waves were breaking over her bows and then, when the wind changed, she was taking on water first from the port side and then from the starboard so that Horace who had taken to his grubby cabin was tossed about until he was violently sick. Of course, there was no washbasin in the steamer so he staggered about in search of a bathroom without any luck and finally vomited over the side while clinging desperately to the ship's rusty guardrails and getting soaked. Below him the tramp seemed not to be making any progress and looking briefly aft he could see no wake, which suggested the engine and with it the propellers had stopped. Had he known anything about ships he would have realised the reason for the ship's wallowing and constant change of direction. And he'd certainly have been more alarmed. Being sick, almost literally, to death, he searched for a bucket and took it down to his cabin to puke into. He wished now he had chosen to come by air. At least if the plane crashed death came quickly. But that had been impossible. He'd have had to produce his passport and the money in his suitcases would most likely have been found.

When the engine started up again and the ship began to move forward into relatively still water, he finally fell asleep.

The next morning Horace emptied the contents of the bucket out the porthole and got out the map of Europe he had bought in London. He had to face up to the fact that he was entirely without sea legs and the thought of enduring another night in such awful conditions and in such a wretched condition was more than he could stomach. He would jump ship at Holland and might still keep his route secret if he carried on the journey via the various railway lines that would be most unlikely for any long-distance traveller to take. But the map was not detailed enough to show any railway lines other than the main ones carrying high-speed trains between large cities.

Cutting his losses, Horace decided to head for Berlin by the most circuitous route he could find. Ditching most of his luggage he disembarked and only got to the city a week after he'd started out from London. On arrival he immediately changed a large sum of pounds into euros at a number of different banks and exchanges. That evening he caught a bus into the eastern part of the city which had been in the Russian zone and spent the night in the cheapest room in the cheapest hotel he could find. He had decided to alternate between buses and trains, and take a zigzag route back out of Germany. Where he would end up he had no idea. His sole object was to prevent anyone tracing him and wherever he stayed he intended to give a different name. Best of all he bought a passport from a drunk Englishman who'd come to Munich to watch a football match and followed this up by buying a second one from a man with a beard in Salzburg. He spent two fruitless days cultivating his whiskers but in the event he didn't have to use either of them to successfully pass the border crossing into Italy.

Chapter 27

At Grope Hall Esmond had no idea what a furore his and Belinda Ponson's disappearance had aroused.

This was partly because he had no way of knowing where he was and partly because he was still recovering from his alcoholic hangover and the sleeping pills he was given each night. They weren't strong ones but they were more than enough to make him dozy. Being called Joe Grope made things worse and having to call Belinda darling instead of auntie didn't make the situation any more comprehensible. Every now and then he climbed off the bed to look out the window in the hope of seeing something he could understand, like houses, only to be confronted by endless fields of rough and tufted grass with, in the far distance, what appeared to be a grey stone wall. Nearer the house there were flocks of sheep munching away and down below the window pigs had turned the ground into a large patch of muddy earth with their snouts and hooves. More alarmingly there seemed to be two black bulls roaming the grounds completely untethered.

There was no sound of the passing cars he was accustomed to in Selhurst Road. Only the occasional gust of wind shook the glass as he stared out. Occasionally he thought he could hear the murmur of voices coming from the room below. One at least seemed to be that of a man because it was deeper and less frequent than that of what he took to be the women, though he couldn't be sure. The floor was too thick and deadened by moss for him to hear much but every now and again he could definitely make out laughter, albeit brief laughter, before the discussion or perhaps the argument resumed.

In fact, what remained of the Grope family – Myrtle and Belinda – were mostly discussing the problem of getting rid of the old Ford Belinda had driven up in from Essexford. It was still in the barn but on the off-chance it was spotted it would provide a very good clue for someone to pass on to the police. Belinda had already removed the number plates with the help of Old Samuel who had obliterated the numbers with the flat head of a large hatchet but getting rid of the car itself was far more difficult.

'We could always drive it down the drift mine and bury it out of sight under tons of soil from the roof,' Old Samuel suggested.

'And where are we going to get the coal we need for the stove if we block the main tunnel to the coal face?' asked Myrtle.

'Oh, there are lots of side tunnels with no coal left in them. All we've got to do is drive into one of those and then bring the roof down.'

'And if someone starts digging through it, what then?'

'Barbed wire. Lots of it,' said Old Samuel, getting quite carried away at the thought of it. 'Rolls of it going back under the roof fall for twenty yards. Of course, we could have a locked iron gate as well to stop people stealing coal.'

'But no one ever comes down past the bulls and the dogs.'

'True, but just in case . . .'

'Anyway, how are you going to bring the roof down?' asked Belinda.

'With explosives.'

'What explosives?'

'Never you mind. You wouldn't want to know,' Old Samuel sniggered. 'But I'm going to need the young fellow's help.'

Excited by the thought of at long last using his stockpile of explosives Samuel hurried from the room tugging the door shut behind him.

Once they knew they were alone the women began to discuss Esmond's future.

'Now about this marriage,' said Myrtle. 'It will take place in the chapel. And if he doesn't give you girl babies, we'll send him back to his mother and father in Croydon and look for another one.'

'Or he can stay on here,' Belinda said hastily, blanching at the thought of Esmond going home and telling either his mother or his Uncle Albert where he had been held captive and who had taken him there. 'We need more men to work the farm and there's lots of space here in between the bulls and the sheep for lurking. Not that he'll have much time for that. What he doesn't know about farming and mining Old Samuel can teach him.'

At this both women cackled loudly and Esmond, listening from above, wondered once again just what the joke could be.

Chapter 28

At Essexford Police Station, Albert needed no teaching: he had already learnt that it didn't pay to demand to have his lawyer present when he was being questioned as a suspected terrorist and a murderer of two people into the bargain.

It was made worse by his lawyer being a former suitor of the woman he was supposed to have killed. The superintendent himself had explained the situation to him and the lawyer had suggested they knock the truth out of 'that shit of a murdering bastard'. The superintendent shared his opinion. No one apart from the police knew that Albert Ponson was in custody. The newspapers were having a field day writing about the presumed explosion at a heavily armoured house and lost no time in linking it with al-Qaeda as a storage place for bomb-making materials.

In the meantime the house had been sheathed in an enormous blue tent and more police had been brought in to keep the public as far away as possible. There were yellow ribbons stretched across the road and men and women in white jumpsuits were examining every inch of the interior. Samples of blood from both the bungalow and the DIY slaughterhouse were undergoing analysis and the extent of gore at the latter site had excited the police into believing that this was a quite appallingly organised crime.

The mixture of various animal bloods made the police work exceedingly difficult. They took samples to the top forensic laboratory where even world-renowned experts found it difficult to distinguish between the DNA of animals and that of slaughtered humans or even those who had merely cut themselves in their amateurish effort to kill their struggling beasts.

'Whoever thought up this conglomeration of blood certainly knew exactly what he was doing. I've never come across anything like it in my life,' said the head of the forensics team.

Much the same could be said for Albert Ponson. He'd never known what it was like to be cross-examined by a superintendent who had come up the hard way from an ordinary copper and who was brutally ambitious.

And who was still suffering twinges from a badly stitched forehead.

'You bloody well wait. I'm going to teach you to kick me in the balls twice,' Albert squealed, after he'd been kicked there the second time.

'Hardly, mate. I won't be around by the time you come out of prison. Like in forty years. Wrap your head around that one, you murderous terrorist! Come to that, you'll be lucky to be released in your own lifetime. We've got some other charges against you.'

'Like what?'

'Like killing two of my men and maiming three others when that roof came down.'

'But I didn't do that!' shouted Albert, seriously worried now. 'I told you the front would come off when you pulled the gate down.'

'Did you now?' said the superintendent and turned to the chief inspector. 'Did he tell you that?'

'Of course he didn't, the lying bastard. He said he couldn't get out and with all that bulletproof metal and glass we couldn't get in. We were just trying to help the sod. And where's his wife and that youngster Esmond, I'd like to know?'

'Dead as like as not. His missus must have known too much and may have tried to blackmail him. He killed her first no doubt, and then he tried to bump his nephew off with an overdose of alcohol. Didn't just try either. Forensic says there was enough vomit on that carpet to kill a hippopotamus. Whisky, brandy, just about every booze, including absinthe, you can think of. Talk about drinking the poor bastard into an early grave.'

'That's a bloody lie,' shouted Albert. 'I never gave the brute any absinthe.'

The superintendent grinned.

'Didn't give him any absinthe. Caught you that time. Meaning you gave him just about every other hard liquor in the house. That would be plenty enough to do his liver in. I know it would finish mine just looking at the empty bottles lying about the floor. Dear God and I've got to go and question the poor lad's loony mother. Just keep this swine awake and go on giving him hell.'

The superintendent left Albert's cell and dawdled down to the hospital, fingering his bandaged forehead. He certainly wasn't looking forward to telling Vera that her darling Esmond had disappeared and was almost certainly dead.

Chapter 29

To his continued befuddlement, Esmond had been set to work at the end of the week. He was helping Old Samuel in the side shaft of the coal mine. 'You bore two holes in the roof with this,' Old Samuel told him, passing over a large hand drill. 'And I'll get the dynamite ready.'

'Dynamite? Where did you get dynamite?'

'Found it. Must have been left over from when they first began to dig for coal. They had to use it because it wasn't possible to get a railway track through the rock. I've kept it dry far away from the Hall where no one would find it.'

'But isn't it dangerous?'

'I reckon not. I sealed it in a watertight container.

171

Anyway, we'll see if it's still good. Now you fetch the stepladder first – you aren't tall enough to reach up there – and then drill two holes in the roof.'

Esmond did as he was told and presently was busy with a drill.

'What's next?' he asked when he'd made the holes Old Samuel wanted.

Old Samuel had fetched a big china basin and was sitting on a box outside ladling gunpowder from the basin into a couple of twelve-bore cartridges from which a thin copper wire protruded. The wire came from a drum and when he had measured fifty yards he knotted the wire together. After that he fetched the sticks of dynamite and with the aid of the ladder put them up in the holes in the roof with the cartridge cases wedged underneath them.

'That ought to do the trick,' he said as they went out into the yard. 'I don't see that rock staying up there much longer. Now stop lurking around the place and go and bring the old Ford down here.'

Esmond was fascinated. He'd always wanted to blow something up. He went back to the barn and fetched the old Ford. It fitted easily into the tunnel and while Old Samuel's back was turned Esmond climbed onto the bonnet and carefully checked that the cases were fully pressed up into the holes he'd drilled. In fact, they fitted exactly and only one of the two needed extra wedging with a sliver of wood. Meanwhile, Old Samuel had fetched an electric generator and was waiting for Esmond, whom he called Joe or Mr Grope, to help him bring down some bales of barbed wire.

'Not that we'll need it but it's best to be on the safe side. We'll explode the roof first to make sure the powder works as it should do. After that we may have to get an iron gate. That will deter people coming in, not that anyone's likely to. Those black bulls keep them away from the house in any case. Oh no, Grope Hall is known for being a place to avoid. From what I've heard in the kitchen you're safe here. Mind you, no man has ever got away from here unless they want him to, "they" being them in the kitchen.'

'I don't want to,' said Esmond, surprising himself with the sudden realisation. He'd always had a hankering for blowing things up and he'd discovered how much he enjoyed looking after the pigs. Above all he felt free. The thought of going back to the house in Croydon sickened him. Out here, wherever 'here' was, he felt he could be himself instead of having his mother suffocating him and calling him her darling, never mind his father attacking him with a carving knife. Looking back over his life he was conscious that he had never for a moment really known who he was. Here in this wild countryside he felt he finally did. Even if he wasn't entirely certain quite what he was called.

'Might as well see if the cartridges work,' said Old Samuel and attached the main copper wire to the electric generator. 'Stand by, I'm going to start it now.'

173

He turned the generator on, and a dull rumble came from the side shaft along with a cloud of powdered earth. When it had cleared they went in and peered at the result of this improvised explosion. There was no sign of the old Ford.

'Better get the flashlight, Joe. It looks as if the whole roof is down. Mind you, that will save us using the barbed wire.'

All the same Old Samuel was taking no chances. That night he painted a large warning notice which read 'DANGER. BEWARE FURTHER ROOF FALLS' and fixed it to a post beside the entrance.

'That ought to do the trick,' he said.

And so for the first time since his arrival, Esmond was given no sleeping pill and slept happily.

Chapter 30

The same couldn't be said of Vera. By the time the superintendent returned to the hospital she was, to put it mildly, distraught but had recovered sufficiently to ask questions and to try to answer some. The inspector, on the other hand, was determined to get his own back for her assault on him and for having ten stitches in his head.

'Keep her in the private room if she's got to stay in hospital and isn't malingering,' he told the doctor. 'She needs to be as far away from the other patients as possible and you need to make sure she can't get out of bed.'

When the doctor asked why this was necessary the superintendent replied, 'She's a suspect in what appears to be a multiple murder case. Certainly a case in which she has to be thoroughly interrogated.'

'Gawd! Multiple murder!' said the doctor, horrified at what he was hearing. 'Who is she supposed to have killed?'

'I'm not in a position to say. Anyway, it's only supposition but the evidence looks like she could have some connection with a serious crime. Oh, and while you're at it, can you give her something to keep her calm?'

The doctor looked at him in bewilderment.

'Something to keep her calm? The woman's . . . God knows what she is. Most of the time she's completely hysterical unless she's wholly sedated.'

'I don't want her to be fully sedated. Give her something that will lessen her anxiety and become relatively reasonable. I don't want any more stitches in my head.'

'Five drops of Rivotril in her tea should do the trick.'

'What the devil's that?'

'It's a benzodiazepine. On the other hand if I give her more right now she could fall asleep. Better leave her alone for half an hour.'

The superintendent kept out of sight in the public waiting area to give her time to settle down before going in to question her.

'Mrs Wiley, I don't want to upset you,' he lied sympathetically, 'but I do want to find out where your son has gone. Perhaps you can help me. Have you any ideas that you haven't mentioned to me?'

Vera stared at him. This was a very different detective to the one she had hurled to the floor. On the other hand his scalp was still bandaged so it must be the same one.

'But I've told you already I don't know what's happening,' she replied. 'That's why I brought him up here to my brother.'

'Because . . . ?' the superintendent began.

'Because my husband tried to kill him and I told you that last time too. Why are you asking me the same questions again?'

'We have to make sure you haven't left anything out accidentally, Mrs Wiley.'

'Of course I haven't. What sort of things would I leave out?'

The superintendent sighed. The bloody woman seemed to have all her wits about her. He began to wish the doctor had given her a strong sedative after all.

'All right, I'll ask you a different question. We've been to your house in Selhurst Road and your husband isn't there. Can you tell me where he might be?'

'In a pub,' snapped Vera, secretly shocked to think she'd forgotten all about Horace still locked in his room and desperately trying to remember when she'd last fed him. 'Anyway, how do you know he's not at home? He may still be in bed.'

'I can assure you he's not.'

'You're telling me you broke in? You had no right to do that,' Vera spat at him. 'You're policemen, you're supposed to be keeping the law not breaking it.'

The chief detective sighed again.

'We did nothing of the kind. The back door hadn't been locked. We simply walked in.'

'You're lying. I always lock up before going out,' protested Vera, forgetting that in fact she had rushed straight out back to her brother's that morning when the phone wasn't answered, fearing the worst and indeed finding it when she got there.

'But perhaps Mr Wiley doesn't.'

'He does. He's a bank manager and he's always been very particular. He's particular about everything in life, including locking all the doors.'

'Not about his clothes he isn't. Two jackets and a suit were lying on the floor. So were some socks. All in all he'd emptied the wardrobe and dumped everything in it on the unmade bed. The inside of the safe at his bank was in the same mess.'

The superintendent paused to let Vera reflect on what this description implied. It was a risky thing to have told her given that it was only partly true but it might provoke her to explain what sort of marriage the Wileys had. He was pretty sure it was a distinctly unsatisfactory one.

Chapter 31

'That'll teach her,' the superintendent said to the sergeant who was hovering nearby when Vera's response to his description of the house and the bank was to go into hysterics for the umpteenth time.

'Make some extremely strong coffee – and I mean extremely strong – so that the bitch doesn't get a wink of sleep tonight. I'm having that carving knife her husband tried to kill his son with brought up from Croydon and I want you to make sure there's plenty of blood on the blade. I intend to get the domestic side of this massacre out of the way before the anti-terrorist squad get onto it.'

'Any reason why they shouldn't, sir? Their forensic

specialists are already working on the blood samples from the bungalow and the slaughterhouse.'

'And not getting anywhere. I want to show them that local police can do just as well or better because we know the area and the crooks better than they do.'

In the ward a little while later, Vera was living up to the promise of that extremely strong coffee and making such a din that the patients on nearby wards were shouting complaints too.

'Better get the woman down to the station,' said the superintendent, 'I'll question her there. And make sure she's handcuffed – I don't want any more stitches in my scalp.'

'Where are you taking me now?' Vera yelled as four burly policemen lifted her off the bed.

'To a nice quiet place where you're going to tell us just where your murderous husband is.'

'In hell I hope. That's where he ought to be.' Then Vera paused before admitting, 'He should be in bed. That's where I left him.'

'Dead or alive, Mrs Wiley?'

'Dead is what he would be if I had my way. Alive of course, you idiot! What on earth are you doing arresting me when my darling boy might be in a ditch or worse?'

At this thought Vera started to wail and beat her head against the cell wall until after an hour she collapsed into a stupor.

'She's going to have heart failure if you go on like

180

this, I warn you,' the doctor who had accompanied Vera to the police station said.

'Best thing for her,' growled the superintendent, who was in favour of hanging. 'Here I am sitting up all damned night and not getting a straight answer out of the wretched woman. I still haven't a clue where her husband's got to.'

'He's probably as far away from her as possible. I know I would in his place. Imagine living with a wife like her,' said the chief inspector.

'I prefer not to. You've checked with the bank of course. Apart from the mess was there any money missing?'

The chief inspector shook his head.

'Not a cent. Whatever the blighter's up to he's been honest there.'

'Have you tried the ports?' asked the doctor.

'Of course we have. He hasn't crossed the Channel, that's for sure. In any case, apparently he doesn't like travelling and he certainly won't fly. Said to be scared of it because he's got a phobia about heights.'

The chief inspector looked at his notes.

'But she said he proposed to her at the top of Beachy Head. Seems a damned odd place to go if you're terrified of heights.'

'Best place when you intend to commit suicide, which after twenty years with that woman would be the natural thing to do.'

'True. So, if she's telling anything like the truth, he proposed to her at the top of a 529-foot cliff – from which people frequently jump to their deaths. And this is a bloke who's said to have a phobia about high places. No way. Someone's lying. Could be either of them or both, though my bet's on her. All that nonsense about the "three hims". I suppose you could interpret that as "hymns", although apparently they've never been near a church on Sunday. But we're straying from the main issue which is where that Mrs Ponson and the lad have disappeared too.'

The superintendent gave a bitter laugh before replying. 'I'd say that bloody abattoir and a mincing machine. Ponson didn't build that beastly slaughter-house for nothing. He'd had a vile purpose for it from the beginning. And it wasn't simply to help small-time local breeders either.'

'I'm with you on that one,' said the chief inspector. 'He's made a bit of money flogging second-hand cars. Or stolen ones. What I don't know is why we haven't found out what he's really been up to.'

'Because the bastard didn't sell stolen cars in his second-hand yard. And I'm certain he didn't nick them himself either. Got other thieves to do that for him and undoubtedly had legitimate deals too. Of course the nicked cars wouldn't be in his own name either and the so-called owner would get his cut of the profits. And a lot less than Ponson you may be sure.' The superintendent turned to the doctor. 'Don't think we didn't try to nail the bugger before now because we did, but he was too fly for us. But thank God we've got the sod now.'

'Of course, al-Qaeda could have recruited him years ago and put up money too,' added the chief inspector.

'What I want to know is where that husband of hers has got to,' said the doctor, who'd found the discussion not only fascinating but also that it helped to keep him awake. 'I'd like to know why he tried to kill his own son too. He sounds as mad as she is.'

Just at that moment a detective who hadn't heard the previous conversation came in.

'We've found a weapon at the Wileys' house, sir. And from the traces of blood on it there's no doubt that someone tried to kill someone else with it,' he said, brandishing a plastic bag with a carving knife inside it.

'Well, at least Mrs Wiley was partly telling the truth,' said the superintendent. He looked at the doctor before saying, 'I'm with you though. I just wonder where her psychopath of a husband has got to.'

Chapter 32

Horace shared his bewilderment. He'd crossed so many frontiers and bought so many maps in languages he couldn't read that he had no idea where he was.

From Germany he'd crossed into Poland, then over the mountains into Slovenia and through the Czech Republic and Austria before getting lost in Trieste. Then from Italy he'd headed towards France, always staying in the most modest hotels and giving a false name. Several times in his effort to stay away from main roads he'd chosen narrow country ones which turned out to have no hotels on them, which meant frequently having to sleep rough. In fact, he was often unable to sleep at all because he seemed to be surrounded by large animals, or at least he imagined he might be, which was just as bad.

Finally, looking like a hobo (he wished to hell he had brought more clothes and an electric razor with a plug that fitted European sockets), he crossed into France. At that point he gave up trying to shave and grew a beard.

About his only consolation through all this was that anyone trying to follow him was going to find it impossible. But that didn't offer much comfort when having walked for days and days across what he thought was probably Italy, Horace found his route blocked by an impossibly wide river. Since he couldn't swim and there was no way he was going to turn round and retrace his steps, he had to walk miles further to find a bridge. His relief at the sight of one was short-lived when he realised that the bridge had a policeman apparently guarding it.

Horace wasn't going to risk a confrontation with the police so that meant waiting on the riverbank until the policeman, whose main duty seemed to be to stop speeding cars and to prevent traffic jams building up on the narrow bridge, was distracted. He waited a good hour until a particularly bad jam involving two large trucks gave him his opportunity and he sauntered past them and across the bridge.

Safely on the far side of the river, still in France, he kept on travelling. One morning, bleary-eyed and tired, he waited for a bus and finally stopped one with a Spanish number plate and climbed aboard. Once seated Horace struck up a conversation with the man beside him and found to his relief that he spoke quite good English.

'Where are you going?' the man asked once they'd exchanged names.

'I've no idea,' admitted Horace. 'But what I'd like to know is what people are speaking around us. I can recognise Spanish but this is different.'

'We're in Catalunya and the people here speak Catalan. It's a mixture of French and Spanish and quite often people use Castilian or Madrid Spanish. Of course, each area has its own accent and that makes it all the more difficult to understand. Under Franco no one was allowed to talk Catalan but of course when they were at home they did. Mind you, the pure Spaniards can't understand a word of it.'

By now Horace felt thoroughly confused and rather than have to continue holding such a bewildering conversation spent the rest of the journey pretending to be asleep.

But his travelling companion was correct. They were in Catalunya and even Horace couldn't fail to recognise the distinctive architecture of Barcelona. By the time they got there, Horace had come to a decision. From what he had seen of the landscape and from what he'd heard before he feigned sleep about how non-violent the Catalans were from the man in the next seat, this might be a good place to pause his

187

journey. He could hire a car and explore the area if they would accept his passport in place of a driving licence. But even if they wouldn't, he was well used to trains and buses and travelling on foot.

Horace booked into the first hotel he came to after leaving the bus, bought some new shoes and yet another map together with a guidebook in English and spent the afternoon in his room planning a sight-seeing route.

He also discovered an old copy of the *Daily Telegraph* in the hotel hall and, having not seen a British newspaper since he began his journey, was delighted to find that there was no mention of a police search for anything to do with the crime he hadn't in any case committed. But best of all, from Horace's point of view, was reading the headline story of how a Mr Albert Ponson's bungalow had collapsed in mysterious circumstances and that the owner was himself under arrest. What Horace didn't know was that his edition of the *Telegraph* was an early one. Had he had access to a later edition or to an evening paper from that same day, he would have seen a very different headline indeed.

Chapter 33

Unknown to Horace, the previous day a series of al-Qaeda bombs had been found in twelve cities across England, though fortunately they were discovered and rendered useless before any damage could be done.

Even so, the whole country was now on the alert for the terrorists much to the delight of the superintendent who had been under pressure to inform Scotland Yard in the clearest terms what the hell he was keeping under wraps in Essexford.

'Just a normal sordid domestic quarrel with a missing wife and a kid of seventeen,' he'd reported back. 'And a jerry-built house that collapsed. The man we've arrested is a car thief suffering from paranoia. We've already had the wreckage searched for any explosives or documents that would indicate any knowledge of bomb-making and there aren't any. And anyway, our bloke's an alcoholic and as far from being a religious fanatic as anyone could be. Check his record if you don't believe me.'

Having kept the anti-terrorist squad away he went back to interrogating Albert Ponson and, more reluctantly, Vera Wiley. She was as difficult to get any sense out of as she had been before.

'I've told you a thousand times, I left him in bed. Ask my brother Al, he'll tell you.'

'He says your husband told him he was going to cut this Esmond son of yours into bits and dissolve him in nitric acid in the fifty-gallon water butt at the back of the house. What do you say to that?'

Vera was past saying anything. As she slumped back in a faint on the bench the superintendent knew he'd gone too far. He got up and left the room. He found the sergeant and told him to go in and deal with the bloody woman who was driving him out of his mind.

'And don't say anything to the bloody woman about her son being missing presumed dead when she comes round.'

'Shall I show her the knife, sir?' the sergeant asked, producing the thing in a plastic bag.

The superintendent held his head between his hands.

'For heaven's sake, that's not a carving knife. It is a chisel, a chisel covered in blood.'

The sergeant looked at it and tried to think what to say.

'I suppose that if one wants to chop a dead body into bits to fit into a water butt filled with nitric acid a chisel is as good as a carving knife. Even better in fact, I mean – '

'Never mind what you mean. I'm telling you that's not the carving knife I was shown and if that's what you use at home to slice bread then by the time you've carved the stuff it must be as stale as a mummified brick.'

The sergeant hurried off and presently returned with the carving knife. The superintendent stared at it furiously.

'Where's the bloody blood on it?' he demanded.

'The inspector said he thought it would be unhygienic to put blood on it. He wanted to use it at home and anyway he didn't think you'd notice . . .'

But the superintendent had had enough.

'You go back in there and see if she's come round yet.'

He went through to Albert's cell only to find that Albert Ponson still wasn't prepared to answer any questions until he had a different solicitor.

'I have no idea where Belinda's gone or that damned youth for that matter. All I know is that they just disappeared. I'm not saying any more unless you get me a better lawyer. And don't give me that bull about the roof falling on the two coppers' feet.

It didn't do anything of the sort. That's why I want my own lawyer and you can ask any questions you like but you're not going to get any answers out of me without him.'

The superintendent gave up. Ponson's attitude almost convinced him that the damned man really didn't have a clue where his wife and Esmond Wiley had got to. Worse still, he had warned the chief inspector that to drag the iron gate open would bring down the front of the bungalow and he hadn't been lying. Thank God no one believed him. What was baffling was Ponson's need to turn the place into a bulletproof fortress in the first place.

As the superintendent drove home from the police station it suddenly dawned on him that the wretched man might be mad and suffering from an extreme form of persecution mania. That would account for the armoured bungalow. And if madness ran in the family it might also account for his sister's conviction that her husband had tried to murder their son. On the other hand, there was that fearful slaughterhouse across the fields. Not that that didn't suggest insanity too, though of a distinctly frightful kind.

Or was he just pretending madness to hide the fact that he was both a crook and a terrorist? But then again the detectives had been over the house on their hands and knees and, apart from the bullet holes around the lock to the kitchen door, there wasn't the slightest molecule of high explosive in the entire place.

The superintendent sighed heavily and turned his car round to drive back to the station.

'I want the entire body of detectives who have been assigned to this case to be assembled here in twenty minutes,' he ordered the desk sergeant.

While mulling over the absence of any evidence that Ponson had been involved in terrorism it had suddenly occurred to the superintendent that the wretched fellow might have been genuinely locked inside his extraordinary house as he claimed. When the detectives arrived he had one question to put to them.

'Have any of you found any keys to the doors of this place?'

No one had.

'Next question: how come nothing electric worked?'

'Someone wrecked the fuse box,' a sergeant told him. 'And I mean smashed it. That's why he was shouting to be let out.'

'And you're only telling me now?' fumed the superintendent. 'Anything else I ought to know? Or would you rather keep it to yourselves?' he asked sarcastically then went on. 'What I'd like to know above all else is exactly where these three people have disappeared to. I want every one of you to concentrate on that from now on until I tell you not to.'

'Three?' said the chief inspector. 'Don't you mean two? Mrs Ponson and the Wiley boy?'

'No, three. You're forgetting Mr Horace Wiley. He's the only person to have shown any real violence if that loony woman's to be believed, and for once I'm beginning to look at it her way. Just suppose he did kill the son? Maybe he thought the murder had been witnessed by Mrs Ponson – she'd have to go too.'

'So where are the bodies?'

'Forget about them for the moment. Once we get Wiley we'll get that out of him even if I have to use thumbscrews. What I want to know now is where that man Wiley is.'

'Could be dead too.'

'Could be anywhere,' said the superintendent miserably.

He'd come to the conclusion that the whole bloody family was probably insane, including the son, murdered or not. And the way things were progressing he would soon be joining them.

That night, unable to sleep, the superintendent lay pondering the case he had taken on. At the time he had imagined it would be a relatively minor one and one that would allow him to arrest Albert Ponson whom he'd had in his sights for years but had been unable to pin a really serious crime on. But now he didn't think so.

On the other hand, the extraordinary armoured bungalow and possible three murdered people raised his hopes of pinning something on Ponson. He couldn't be certain that they had been murdered but they'd all undoubtedly disappeared and as his sleepless night wore on the more the superintendent came to believe and certainly hope that the DIY slaughterhouse had been used for something more than killing cattle and pigs. Forensics admitted there wasn't sufficient human blood in the ghastly place to lead them to a definite conclusion but they did think that people could well have been strangled there. As the night wore on the inspector's macabre hopes grew. Why, for instance, had the place never been scrubbed down but blood had been allowed to coagulate so that it was almost as hard as the concrete of the floor and wall? Surely that was Ponson sending a warning of what he was prepared to stoop to where his enemies were concerned?

Against that there was the counter-evidence that no murder involving bloodshed had been committed there, and even the superintendent had to admit that claiming strangulation as the cause of death was rather clutching at straws.

But what about the bullets at the bungalow? Could they really just be Ponson trying to get out of the locked house as he claimed?

A moment later the superintendent had been forced back unhappily to the conclusion that he was dealing with nothing more than three missing persons. Worse still, he might be held responsible for the destruction of that bungalow. Although if he could just find

Horace Wiley he might still have a good chance of promotion.

It was nearly four o'clock before he finally fell asleep, just two hours before he needed to be up and facing the whole bloody nightmare all over again.

Chapter 34

On the coast in south Barcelona, Horace was having a delightful time. The hotel he'd found was excellent and he had booked a room overlooking the beach which was densely packed with sunbathers. To Horace's amazement many of the women lying on the beach were wearing costumes that were skimpy to a point he wouldn't have believed possible.

Several hundred metres beyond the open area where people were swimming there was a row of buoys where yachts, speedboats and some larger dinghies were anchored.

Horace sat on the balcony outside his room and stared down happily. He was perfectly content with the view from the hotel: he didn't want to be on the crowded beach sunbathing, and in any case, he couldn't swim. Behind him there were the faint sounds of the maid as she vacuumed his room and made the bed.

Earlier, after a perfect breakfast in the dining room where he had a table near the window, the manager of the hotel who spoke good English had asked him if he wanted an English paper. Horace had said he'd like one but expressed his surprise that he could get one in Spain.

'In Catalunya, señor,' said the manager pleasantly, 'they come every day in the summer. In winter you have to go into the town. It isn't far but we're shut for a month in January to give the waiters a holiday. The paper shop is down in the plaza now and you'll get one there.'

Horace thanked him and watched while he went to another table and spoke in Catalan and then in pure Spanish to a couple who evidently didn't understand and replied in very good English that they were from Finland.

'Finland,' said the manager and asked if they had chosen what they would like for breakfast. But Horace had lost interest and went out onto the seafront. He found the newspaper shop where he bought the *Daily Telegraph* and, for a change, the *Daily Mail*.

On his return he'd come up to his room and now he sat on the balcony without looking at the papers. A white cruise liner on the horizon caught his attention and he was just regretting he hadn't chosen that comfortable way of escaping rather than the awful voyage to Latvia and the journey across Europe when he remembered he had taken the route he had via the London docks for fear that the regular ports could well have been watched and he might well have been recognised. In any case, he reflected, on a cruise liner there was also the chance of meeting one of his bank's customers. No, the tramp steamer had been the safest, if most uncomfortable, way of crossing into Europe.

All Horace needed now was to completely change his appearance. He had already grown a moustache and his beard was coming along nicely. It would more than match the one in the passport he had bought in Salzburg.

Finally Horace turned to the newspapers he had bought and went through them thoroughly to check if there was any mention of a missing bank manager from Croydon and, worse still, his photograph. Much relieved at finding nothing of the sort, he resumed his studies of the bodies below him on the sand and wished he was still a young man.

Chapter 35

Esmond's feelings were quite the reverse of his father's in that he finally felt grown-up. He was enjoying himself hugely learning about running the estate with Old Samuel and was at last being treated like an adult and given adult responsibilities. He had grown very fond of the pigs and piglets rooting in the space between the vegetable garden next to the house and the high stone wall with the archway, with its great iron gate that they had driven the old Ford Cavalier through when they had buried it in the old drift mine. Then there was the milking shed with a stone-walled track that led down from the fields away across the grassy slopes. Esmond, or Joe Grope as everyone insisted on calling him, enjoyed driving the cows down to the shed just as he enjoyed everything he was told to do.

He had no idea where he was but he didn't care. For the first time in his life he was not being mollycoddled by his mother or so patently hated by his father. To complete his sense that he had escaped the divided self-uncertainty he had suffered all his previous life, Wiley by name had gone for ever although wily by nature remained. In bed that night Esmond considered the future and knew exactly what he was going to do.

Chapter 36

In Essexford, the superintendent was in despair. The new forensic specialist shipped in by the Home Office had been patronising and not in the least helpful, though he had identified Esmond's DNA on the carpet of the bungalow where Albert claimed he had fallen and had further demonstrated Esmond's relationship with Mrs Wiley by way of blood extracted in a syringe from his mother's arm.

'Sure, so we know they're mother and son but there's not enough of his blood on the floor to justify any suggestion that he's been murdered. There's glass all over the place. He could have tripped on a bottle. Were all these broken bottles here when you broke in?'

'Yes,' said the superintendent bitterly, not liking the inflection the forensic specialist put on the words 'broke in'. 'I hope you don't think my men raided the off-licence and got plastered. They aren't that dumb.'

The forensic specialist shook his head and kept his thoughts to himself. He had an extremely low opinion of the uniformed branch at the best of times and the Essexford lot who had brought a bulldozer up simply to open a garage door and get into a house had to be the worst he'd ever come across.

'Is there anything else you want me to look at?' he asked, as he moved towards his car making a mental note to tell the Home Office not to waste his time in future.

The superintendent seized his opportunity. He was still smarting over the forensic specialist's arrogance.

'There's just one other building I'd like you to check out,' he said, and led the way down the track to the DIY slaughterhouse. He'd had the sign KILL & EAT YOUR OWN removed from the main road but had kept the one nailed to the wooden side panel next to the DIY slaughterhouse. He knew that neither forensics team spoke to one another and intended to give the specialist a better understanding of that swine Ponson's murderous tendencies and explain why it had been necessary to use the bulldozer to break into the house. He succeeded.

'Dear God, the man must be an absolute sadist,'

the specialist muttered as he read the sign on the building.

'Have a look at the floor inside and tell me something new,' said the superintendent. 'You'll find all the blood samples you need.'

He waited by the door. 'This will give the arrogant bastard something to do,' he thought to himself and accidentally on purpose kicked over a bucket of water onto hard dry blood on the concrete. By the time the man he had come to detest had walked the length of the building the area near the door had a look of authentically fresh blood about it. The forensic specialist then added some of his own to it by slipping on the wet surface and hitting his head on the concrete. Before he could get to his feet he fell twice more and gave vent to his feelings in particularly foul language.

'I'd better see if I can get you some Elastoplast,' said the superintendent and hurried back to the remains of the bungalow.

'And an ambulance: I may have concussion!' shouted the forensic specialist before slowly slumping slightly more comfortably onto the grass under the board that read 'DIY SLAUGHTERHOUSE'. He was beginning to understand how very appropriate the sign was.

Chapter 37

Meanwhile, Vera had been released from the police station and returned to the hospital where, in an isolated and soundproofed private room, she was being interviewed by a psychiatrist who found her exceedingly difficult to analyse.

This was not surprising given the strain Vera had been under for so many days coupled with her increasing conviction that her darling boy had been murdered. In short, she had reverted to the appalling language of the trashy romances that had filled her mind for so many years. As a result when the psychiatrist asked her if she had a happy marriage she answered that her darling husband was the sweetest man she had ever met. The shrink consulted the transcript of her earlier interrogations and read that she had accused Horace of attempting to murder her darling son Esmond with a carving knife ('darling' was a word he had come to detest) and was at a loss to understand her change of attitude. To add to his confusion, Vera claimed that before they had been married she and her fiancé had danced until dawn before making love on the rocks beside the sea and under the moon.

Unwisely he'd asked if she meant they had had sex.

'You disgusting creature,' she screamed at the hapless psychiatrist. 'I said we made love and I meant "love" not "sex" and you had to ask a completely different and horrid question.'

The psychiatrist tried to apologise but Vera wasn't prepared to listen to him or to answer any more of his stupid questions. Half an hour later he gave up the struggle against her silence and left her weeping as the heroines of her books did so frequently when the men they loved rode away on black horses with their shirts open in the dawn.

'I'm damned if I know what to make of her,' he told the superintendent. 'She seems to have a fixation on Barbara Cartland-type novels. Not that I've read one of the rubbishy things myself.'

'You don't think she was just having you on?'

'I don't know what to think. She said her darling husband was the sweetest man she'd ever known.'

'That's the very opposite of her statement to me.

She accused the man of trying to murder their son with a carving knife.'

'I know. I checked her previous statements and they contradicted everything she was prepared to say to me and that was little enough. In my opinion she's either a consummate liar or lives in a fantasy world, and I'm not sure I can help any further with the case.'

The superintendent sighed. He still hadn't recovered from his almost totally sleepless night, let alone from the bloody incident with the forensic specialist at the slaughterhouse.

'Do you think she's a schizophrenic or a psychotic?' he asked.

'I don't know what she is,' the psychiatrist began, 'but if it's any help to you I'd say she is off her rocker and ought to be committed into a mental hospital.'

The superintendent smiled.

'That's all I need to know. Thank you very much. I've got enough on my hands without an utterly insane woman.'

That afternoon Vera, heavily sedated, was carried to an ambulance and driven to a clinic in Suffolk.

Chapter 38

For the first few days at the hotel, Horace spent most of his time on his balcony overlooking the beach and gazing out beyond the red buoys to the yachts of all sizes. The buoys were a couple of hundred metres out from the beach and he realised quite soon that they allowed the people sunbathing to cool off in the seawater and swim in safety. It was August and there was hardly any space left on the beach for newcomers. What amazed him was that there was evidently none of the trouble or the arguments that there would undoubtedly have been if this was a seaside resort in England. Here there might be verbal squabbles but since he didn't understand a word of Catalan or Spanish he was happily oblivious to them.

Besides, he was less interested in the men who from time to time strutted up and down the sands showing off their muscles than in the women. Lying out of sight on the balcony in the shade of the canopy above, he could study their virtually naked bodies through a pair of binoculars he'd bought in a shop in the neighbouring small industrial town. In fact, in some cases he could see that there was no need for the 'virtually'. There they were, lying on their stomachs and only putting bikinis on when they went into the water. Horace Wiley, whose only, thankfully brief, experience of sex had been with Vera after their marriage, was conscious of a sudden surge of lust. It came as an embarrassing surprise to a man who had deliberately suppressed any sexual inclinations to keep his loathsome wife at bay. In any case Horace had been brought up in a family in which anything even faintly erotic was strictly forbidden. As his father had drummed into him, his role in life was solely to make and manage money and to keep the wolf from the door. 'That's what I have done,' he had said repeatedly. 'Unlike that lascivious cousin of mine. Even his father wished he had died at birth.'

But now that he was away from England and could gaze at the most desirable women he had ever seen, his natural feelings so long suppressed came to the fore. He was in the prime of life and he wanted to get into bed with a naked woman and make the most passionate love to her. He wasn't going to waste time wondering what passionate love was; he'd simply do whatever came into his body's 'mind'. The real problem was going to be finding a woman who wanted him to maul her breasts and kiss the most unlikely and possibly the most unhygienic places.

There had to be a nymphomaniac girl on that beach. But how to discover her? He could hardly go down and ask each one that attracted him. She might be married and the last thing he wanted was a furious husband threatening to smash his head in. He gave up and went down to the bar and ordered a strong whisky while he considered the problem. There was a good-looking woman sitting behind him with a strange look in her eyes. She greeted him with a *bon dia* and looked pleased when he replied in English.

'I thought you were an *inglese* by the cut of your clothes,' she said and crossed over to join him. 'Besides, you ordered a Scotch. The natives don't usually drink whisky.'

'Can I offer you one too?'

'Of course. I'll have the same as you.'

'It's a Glenmorangie and a strong one,' he warned her.

'I thought so. You've got good taste. There's nothing I like better. I can't stand gin, even Sapphire Blue. My late husband enjoyed dry Martinis made with it but I've always stuck to whisky. Are you married?'

'I used to be but now I'm free. Thank goodness.'

'A bitch?'

213

'You could call her that. She was . . . well, never mind what she was. Let's just say she was a nightmare to live with.'

'My old man was a bloody brute. Used to knock me about something horrible. My name's Elsie, by the way, and you are?'

'Bert. Are you staying here?'

'I rent my house in summer and I stay in the hotel.'

There was a pause while Elsie looked round the bar. There was no one else there.

'If you come up to my room I'll show you what that bastard husband of mine did to me.' She pulled back her blouse and Horace glanced at a large breast.

'Which floor?' he asked.

'Oh, I'm right at the top and at the back.'

'In that case we'll go to mine. It's one floor up and the view is better. Anyway, I've got another bottle of this stuff up there.'

They went up in the lift and Horace was surprised that Elsie nestled up close to him although there was no one else with them. As they entered his room he was even more surprised when she locked the door. The next moment she'd taken her blouse off and was busy removing her bra. He gaped at her and groped for the Glenmorangie. She stopped him.

'That's for afterwards,' she said.

He sat down on the bed. The whisky was taking effect.

'What do you mean, afterwards?' he gasped. 'After what?'

214

'After what we've both been longing for. You don't imagine for a moment that I don't know what effect a pair of binoculars staring every day at semi-naked girls and practically salivating over them can have? Oh yes, two people can buy binoculars. I followed you and was watching you when you bought them and the moment you came out I went in and bought an even more powerful pair.'

She laughed as he stared at her.

'But where were you? I didn't see you.'

'Of course you didn't. Look over there at that red umbrella. I cut a hole in it and I look through it every day with a towel over my legs to keep the sun off.'

Horace stared at her even more intensely. She was lying on the bed with only her panties on.

'Why did you pick on me?' he said.

She smiled. 'Because you're an innocent, my dear. Because you are a typically English innocent – and shy with it. One thing I am certain of: you're not going to hurt me. I've had enough of sadism. Now get undressed and we'll make love.'

Horace went into the bathroom, had a quick shower and came out naked and pink. As they clasped each other and Elsie squeezed his scrotum gently, Horace had his first glorious orgasm for many years. He rolled off her and knew he had fallen in love. By the time they went down to an excellent lunch he was made happier still by the knowledge that he finally knew what passionate love was and that Elsie's room was not far away.

Chapter 39

At Grope Hall, Esmond was happy too and was busy plotting to ensure that this new-found happiness continued. His previous existence had nothing to offer compared with his new life here. He could scarcely believe he was the same person when he thought back to that insipid fellow lurking around the place and imitating his weakling of a bank manager father for want of anything better to do.

The one thing that still puzzled him was the prospect of having to marry his Aunt Belinda. He wasn't at all sure that he really wanted to and, moreover, he really didn't understand why, or even how it could be done.

Despite Belinda's claim of having divorced his uncle he was sure she was still married. Besides, she was a lot older than he was – she must be in her late thirties or even forty – and he'd always imagined he would marry someone his own age and not someone who was actually old enough to be his mother.

Belinda had said they'd get married in the little chapel by the rose garden. He'd been into it several times and it was quite pretty with three stained-glass panels above the altar – not a bad place to get married at all. Something about the single grave in the chapel did puzzle him. It was longer than any grave he'd ever seen in a church and the gravestone had sunk several inches at one end. It was strange, but then everything at Grope Hall was odd. The fact remained she was almost certainly still married to that drunkard Uncle Albert. If he wasn't her husband and they had got divorced he was sure his mother would have mentioned it.

If they were still husband and wife then Belinda would be committing bigamy if she took another husband and that was a crime. He'd learnt that from his father who had been doing the crossword in *The Times* several years before. He had tried 'bigot' but that was too short and 'bigotry' which had been too long. Finally he had found what he needed in 'bigamy'.

'What's bigomy, Dad?'

'It's spelt with an "a" not an "o", boy. And if it were not a crime I would happily commit bigamy to get away from . . . Oh, never mind. Go and find something to do. Life's difficult enough with your mother around, the last thing I need is you lurking around the place.'

On the other hand, Esmond really didn't want to have to go home again. He liked life at Grope Hall and enjoyed working on the thousands of acres around it. He felt himself to be a power in the land he was supposed, as Joe Grope, to run. He was absolutely certain that there were more advantages to be had from his new name if only he could think of exactly what they might be. And of course if he could make sure that neither Belinda nor that old hag Myrtle got in the way of his plans.

The key thing was that he definitely didn't want to go back to Croydon – or, worse still, to Essexford – and to the suffocating sentimentality of his mother, let alone his mad and murderous father.

Lying on his side beside the piglets' run, Esmond found his thoughts strangely returning to the consequences of bigamy. As Joe Grope married to Belinda, might he be in a position to have her sent to prison for bigamy? And actually, now he came to think of it, for kidnapping him as well? After all, he hadn't asked to come out to this empty landscape. He'd been too drunk at the time – in fact, he'd been unconscious.

The more Esmond thought about it, the better he liked his power and position and the more he liked his plan. He'd go through with the marriage and once that was over he'd put the boot into Belinda. To add to his innocence and her guilt, she had stolen the car and had then insisted it was buried in the coal mine. And Myrtle had collaborated, by ordering Esmond and Old Samuel to carry out the crime.

With a degree of confidence in himself he had never felt before, Esmond crept close to the wall surrounding the yard and made his way unseen until he was under the kitchen window where he could hear what was being said inside.

Over the past few days the Hall had seen the arrival of a number of men and women carrying enormous amounts of luggage which Old Samuel had had to carry up to various of the Hall's bedrooms. None of the new arrivals had much time for Esmond, however, and in fact each time he came into a room the heated discussions they seemed to be engaged in with Belinda and Myrtle came to an abrupt halt. Everyone then looked at him with barely concealed anger until he felt so uncomfortable he had to leave the room.

From his position under the wall Esmond at last began to understand just what the quarrels were about. It seemed that Belinda was claiming that she was next in line to inherit Grope Hall from Myrtle and to be the matriarch of the Grope family, but that these relations, or at least the women relations, were disputing it.

Things had definitely reached crisis point and as Esmond listened he found it difficult to distinguish who exactly was speaking amid all the shrieking.

But from the sound of it he guessed that Belinda had won her argument.

'I wouldn't come back here if you paid me,' yelled one nameless outraged Grope. 'The place is miles from anywhere and there isn't even any central heating.'

'Quite right,' fumed another. 'The thought of living in this hole was so awful I married the first man I met in Potters Bar when I got off the train south. Anyone who imagines I'm going to land up here is out of her mind.'

'But the house ought to be mine!' cried another. 'I spent every childhood here and I've always loved it. All it wants is a bit of love and care and a wife and mother at the helm to look after it.'

'In that case,' Belinda said waspishly, 'perhaps you'll stay around and act as my best woman when I get married to Joe on Friday?'

Esmond's gasp on hearing this almost gave his hiding place away. Friday! Gawd, he was going to be a married man by the end of the week.

Fortunately the noise he made was hidden by the sound of the assortment of angry Gropes banging the door loudly behind them as they left the Hall for good.

Belinda enjoyed her triumph for a moment before going to look for Old Samuel to see if he knew where the nearest Reverend Grope had his parish. Although she had spoken in anger now she came to think of it there wasn't any reason that she shouldn't get married sooner rather than later.

'The Reverend Grope?' Samuel said, looking puzzled. 'That would be Theodore but I don't know that he's got a parish any more. He had a church in some village up Corebate way but he's getting on so I don't know if he's still there. You could try the post office and they might find out for you.'

Belinda smiled to herself. If the reverend was getting on in years it might suit her purpose very well. Perhaps she could persuade him that the banns had long since been read and that there was nothing at all unusual in the age gap between the bride and her groom.

Chapter 40

At the mental hospital Vera Wiley was still in an isolated room to save the other patients from her hysterical screams while also providing the psychiatrists who had been called in to examine her the privacy they supposed they would need. They were quickly disillusioned. There was no need for privacy, discretion or even further questions. Although four expert shrinks came separately to make their own assessment of her they went as a group to give their diagnosis to the superintendent.

'The woman is totally insane,' they said in unison.

'I thought so myself. Can you explain the cause? I mean, what's made her go off her head. She's a mature woman and she's been running a house and brought up a son. Suddenly she flips her lid in this extra-ordinary fashion. Do you reckon she's taken to drugs or something of that sort?'

'All we know is that she suffers from the most ghastly hallucinations and is in a state of terror. She is utterly convinced her husband is a murderer who has killed her son.'

'We've checked on Mr Wiley but can find no trace of him,' said the superintendent. 'And in fact if anyone's been murdered, I'm more inclined to think he has. After all, he seems to have been a thoroughly respectable bank manager up until his disappearance and it's not as if there's any money missing from the bank.'

In the end the psychiatrists unanimously recommended that Mrs Wiley had to stay in the mental hospital and remain there for the rest of her life.

'And would you mind checking on her brother Albert Ponson while you're about it?' the super-intendent asked. 'To my way of thinking he's insane too. He's certainly a long-time crook but it seems to me that he must have an extreme persecution complex. Come up to his bungalow after you've interviewed him and see what I mean for yourselves.'

After they had viewed the remains of the fortress and been shown the DIY slaughterhouse, the psychiatrists shared his opinion. Albert's future was definitely the same as his sister's, though in a different mental hospital of course.

Chapter 41

In his room in the Catalan hotel, Horace Wiley was having a wonderful time. He had made love in a few hours more times than he had in his entire married life, and while he was now so exhausted he could no longer achieve yet another orgasm, he still had an erection and could fondle his lover's buttocks and kiss her breasts to his heart's delight.

Eventually, and with some reluctance, he broke off to go downstairs to the dining room with Elsie. Lunch was a splendid affair since after all his lovemaking Horace found that he had a huge appetite. He devoured a large plateful of Iberian ham and followed it with an enormous pork cutlet and finally a double ice cream and three coffees. Feeling pleasantly full,

Horace and Elsie left the dining room and returned to his bedroom. Horace had just undressed and was about to climb onto the bed with the thought that this was heaven when he slumped to the floor with a terrible thump. Elsie jumped out and knelt beside him to feel his pulse. To her horror she couldn't find one in his wrist or neck. Horace Wiley was dead.

Ten minutes later Elsie had dressed and, having checked that there was no one in the corridor, was about to scurry off to her own room when she realised the bed was in a desperately crumpled state that would indicate all too obviously what had caused his heart failure. It looked exactly as though two people had been making the lethal love on it that Horace and Elsie had. So many people had seen them at lunch together that it seemed certain that she would be implicated.

Elsie relocked the door using a handkerchief and made the bed before turning back to Horace. If she could get him back onto the bed, preferably with his clothes on, the situation would be far safer for her. In fact, considering the enormously fatty lunch he'd had, his death might seem perfectly natural.

But Elsie's attempt to get Horace back into his trousers and shirt failed hopelessly. He was far too heavy. Exhausted by her efforts, she sat down on a chair to get her breath back and only now started to feel the frightful effect of his sudden death.

She was distracted from her grief, however, when

she spotted Horace's briefcase which he'd bought in Barcelona under the clothes cupboard where he had evidently hidden it. Crossing the room she pulled it out and found that it was unlocked. Curiosity got the better of Elsie and she opened the briefcase and examined its contents.

In fact, the only item inside the case was a large brown envelope with a number of what felt like soft-backed notebooks in it. Elsie prised the staples off the end of the envelope and slid the contents out. As she had suspected from feeling the envelope they weren't notebooks but passports, quite a number of them in fact, and a driver's licence.

Elsie examined the driver's licence and opened the passports one at a time, studying the names and the photographs. She recognised her dead lover on the licence immediately as Horace Wiley without the beard. The man with the beard was an Austrian called Hans Bosmann and the passport wouldn't have been much use in six months' time because it would be out of date.

But why would Horace have told her that his name was Bert and why did he have all these obviously false passports? Being a sensible woman Elsie refused to read any British newspapers printed in Spain, even *The Times* and the *Telegraph*, because she wasn't the least bit interested in politics. She read only *La Vanguardia* and *El Pais*, which stuck for most of the time to what was going on in Spain and local affairs.

All the same, the name Wiley seemed somehow familiar and now that she came to think of it she was sure that it had cropped up when she had heard English bathers mention something called the Wiley Mystery. Perhaps the licence she held had something to do with the mystery.

For a moment Elsie thought of leaving the licence with the body before deciding against it. After all, Bert – or Horace as she now knew – was the first man for a long time to have given her so much sexual satisfaction. As she unlocked the bedroom door and dashed up to her own room, she took the licence with her. The passports she left behind.

Horace Wiley had wanted to remain anonymous in life and being dead he would remain so.

Chapter 42

Old Samuel's suggestion that Belinda try the parish in a village near Corebate for a priest who could and would conduct her marriage to Esmond had paid off. Of the Reverend Theodore Grope there was no trace and in fact rumour had it that he had shuffled off somewhere and that he was so ancient that somewhere might be off this mortal coil altogether. But fortunately there was a new incumbent in place and one who seemed to believe her when she told him that everything was in order for the forthcoming nuptials.

Nevertheless, Belinda had had to put up a considerable sum of money ostensibly for the restoration of the village church which was badly in need of repairs.

In the end she had paid happily. In the absence of Theodore she had been worried about getting a parson to come to Grope Hall but the Rev. Horston who was obviously new to the district was happy to do so.

Belinda had also found a smart suit that fitted Esmond well enough. The suit had belonged to a young Grope who had been called up during the war. It was said that he went into the army quite willingly to escape from the boredom of life at the Hall, but it was also said that the poor man had been blown to bits at El Alamein which can't have been quite the escape he was anticipating. Belinda had had to buy Esmond a new pair of shoes and a wedding ring but in the circumstances didn't much begrudge the expense.

With these preparations in hand she set about training her fiancé on the ritual of the marriage. She was astonished how easy it was. Esmond no longer seemed in the least surprised at the prospect. On the contrary, he seemed to be truly delighted to be getting married to her.

'Which only goes to show how young and attractive I must seem to him. And what a delightful boy he is,' she thought to herself misguidedly. 'He doesn't even mind being called Mr Grope.' She herself had started using a distant cousin's maiden name but soon would be Mrs Grope and in control of the Hall and the estate.

Next morning, Esmond got up incredibly early and

went to talk to Old Samuel whom by now he both liked and trusted. He found him sitting outside his cabin over the wall at the top of the hill where it was well out of sight of the Hall.

'I've come to ask you a question,' he said, and sat down on the grass nearby.

'Go ahead. Ask away.'

'Why do they call you Old? You're not old.'

Samuel nodded and lit an ancient pipe.

'You're an observant young fellow, you are. There's no doubt about that,' he said with a grin, not liking to point out that Esmond had asked him this when they first met and actually almost every day since. In fact, he wondered if the young fellow had some kind of brain damage which would explain why he'd stuck around so long. On the other hand, he was starting to like and trust Esmond and so he explained as he had to Belinda that in fact his real name was Jeremy and that, yes, he was only in his mid-thirties.

'You're a good sort, young Joe,' Old Samuel finished up with. 'And blokes like you have been in short supply around here these past few years. Old Myrtle can die in peace now that she knows the estate is in Belinda's hands. Now it's Belinda's turn to worry about the female line.'

'Is that why I'm going to be married?'

'I reckon so,' said Old Samuel. 'Mind you, your future wife is a good-looker which is more than can be said for most of the Grope women. All the same,

I'd watch how you go. You never know what the Gropes are up to. She mightn't have much use for you once you've done your duty, so to speak.'

Esmond smiled. 'I think I'll be all right. I've a few plans of my own, and if I succeed, so will you. You and me are a good team, Old Samuel. And I'd like to call you Young Jeremy from now on if it's all the same to you.'

Samuel smiled back and reached out to shake Esmond's hand.

'Of course it is. Only not in the missus' hearing maybe? You're a good friend, Joe, and for my part I'm going to do my best to watch out for you,' he said. 'I won't let you down if I can help it.'

Esmond climbed over the wall on the furthest side of the field from Samuel's cabin and ran down to where he couldn't be seen from the Hall to spend a little while thinking about this new friendship – perhaps his first ever true friendship even if he couldn't call Young Jeremy by his proper name in public just yet. All that was going to change, though, once he took his rightful place as the owner and boss of the Grope estate.

Before long he heard Belinda calling for him in the distance so he ran back to the house and, avoiding the kitchen, climbed up the stone staircase to the bedroom where he pretended to be just getting dressed when Belinda came in.

'How did you sleep?' she asked.

'Perfectly well. Actually, I had a very nice dream about you. It was about living with you after we're married.'

Belinda was charmed. He really was a delightful youth.

'Only two days to go now,' she said and kissed him before going down to the kitchen to make his breakfast.

Behind her, Esmond smiled to himself. Little did she guess. The two days couldn't pass too quickly for him.

After he'd eaten he went out again and along the railway line until he was round a curve that was once more out of sight of the Hall. Then he sat down in the sun and went over yet again what he was going to say to Belinda once they were married. And how long he should wait before he carried out his threat. He decided he'd wait for a week to let Belinda assume she was still the boss of the estate and then he'd strike. He'd tell her that unless she gave him total control he would have her prosecuted for bigamy. And for kidnapping. And probably for poisoning him with alcohol too.

He was sure that she'd break. But what if she didn't? She might turn nasty and dangerous. He had to take that possibility into account. Well, then he'd disappear and scare the wits out of her by leaving a note suggesting he was going to the police. Yes, that was the answer if she wasn't intimidated by his threats. In any case, he couldn't really believe she'd turn nasty.

After all, she'd saved him from that swine Uncle Albert and from his own murderous father and domineering mother and he was certainly grateful for that.

He lay back in the sun and wondered what his parents were doing. Not that he much cared. He'd turned away from the past and was now concentrated on the future, his future as the first male Grope to be head of the family and in total control of the estate.

It was an extraordinary prospect and a challenging one. But the first thing was to go through with the wedding. Once he and Belinda were married he could force her to do exactly what he wanted.

After two hours Esmond climbed the side of the railway bank and up the hill beyond to the thick pine wood that straddled the top. He'd never been there and he wondered when the trees had been planted. He walked a bit further and suddenly came to a large clearing with a stone wall around it. To his astonishment it was a graveyard. He climbed over the wall and looked at the names on the gravestones. They were nearly all those of Grope women who had run the Hall for many hundreds of years. It occurred to Esmond that if he succeeded with his plan he'd be buried here too when he died. The thought did not depress him in the least. Rather it delighted him. The cemetery was filled with wild flowers and shrubs in bloom but there was no sign that anyone had visited it recently. He wondered why the person who had been buried in the long grave in the chapel had been buried there and not here with all the others. It was much nicer here with a view of all the surrounding countryside and no one much to disturb you.

Esmond looked at his watch and saw it was time for lunch. He climbed back over the wall and hurried back through the trees and twenty minutes later he was in the kitchen. To his amazement in the middle of the old deal table there was a splendid wedding cake. Belinda smiled at him.

'I thought we'd do things properly,' she said. 'I ordered it yesterday and drove into Wexham today to collect it while you were out. After all, tomorrow is Friday.'

'Good Lord, I must be getting absent-minded. I thought you said today was Wednesday. Anyway, that's wonderful,' said Esmond. 'So tomorrow we'll be Mr and Mrs Grope.'

'Of course, darling,' she said and kissed him more passionately than he'd ever been kissed before. 'Now eat your lunch. We're going to have a gorgeous honeymoon.'

'Honeymoon? Where are we going?'

'Nowhere, my love, we'll have it here. Gropes have never gone away from the Hall when they got married. That's the tradition and we must continue it.'

'Oh definitely,' said Esmond who had every intention of doing exactly the opposite. After lunch he went up to his room and wrote the note about going to the police if she turned really nasty about his becoming the head of the Hall. He put it in an envelope which he sealed with superglue and took out with him to look for Old Samuel. He also wanted to ask Young Jeremy to be his best man next day.

After searching high and low he finally found him in the chapel. To Esmond's amazement Old Samuel appeared to be using a carjack under the end of the long brass gravestone set into the floor. He already had it raised eighteen inches and he was busy filling the gap beneath with stones from the disused railway.

'Take a look at this,' he said. 'I've always known there was something very weird about this gravestone.'

Esmond peered down and saw the feet of a skeleton with the end of a spade beside them.

'Weird is hardly the word,' he muttered. 'He isn't even in a coffin. And why is he buried here and not up in the graveyard with all the other Gropes? Do you think he was someone special?'

'Could have been, I suppose, though why they put this great slab of brass on top puzzles me.'

'Possibly to stop him getting out,' said Esmond.

'Or he had it put there to stop the Grope women from getting at him,' smirked Old Samuel.

Esmond wasn't sure he understood the joke but went on. 'Anyway, Young Jeremy, I came to ask if you'd be my best man tomorrow.'

'Sure, though rather you than me. I wouldn't marry a Grope no matter how attractive she was. And don't forget to call me Old Samuel when the women are about else you'll be for it.'

'Don't worry about me. Like I told you, I've got plans.'

'Yes and this fellow probably had his plans as well,' said Old Samuel with a grin, pointing down at the grave. He let the jack down and the brass plate fell back into place. 'Well, I'd better make things spick-and-span in here if the wedding is tomorrow or it'll be my grave I'm digging next.'

Chapter 43

The next morning, a messenger arrived before breakfast with a letter from the Rev. Horston to say that as he had six weddings to conduct that day he would conduct that of Mr Grope and Miss Parry at nine o'clock in the evening or possibly later. He apologised profusely for the delay this would undoubtedly cause them.

'What a nuisance,' said Esmond when he came down dressed in his suit and wearing his new shoes, but his aunt and fiancée did not agree.

'After six weddings he'll be exhausted and won't remember ours at all clearly. That is bound to be an advantage to us.'

'I can't imagine why,' said Esmond.

'Because he'll be in a hurry and won't ask too many questions about our religious beliefs like whether we're members of the Church of England or atheists. That sort of thing. I mean, do you know if you've ever been baptised?'

'Good Lord no. I wouldn't remember in any case. Can you recall what happened when you had only recently been born? If you can you must have a superb memory. Anyway, I'm going for a walk.'

'You're always going for walks,' commented Belinda. 'I can't think why.'

'Because I find the estate interesting. I'm a great lover of wildlife and the countryside. I used to go up to the woods on Croham Hurst with my father before he became an alcoholic and went mad and tried to stab me. There was a sort of very steep gravel path called Breakneck Hill that I liked to slide down. My father seemed to like me to slide down it too.' Esmond paused, lost in the memory of a time that now seemed very far distant before adding, 'In any case, I need to get some exercise. I'd die of boredom sitting around the house all day.'

'Oh, go for your walk then. I can't have you dying of boredom. In fact, I'd come with you but I have lots of things I must do in the house.'

Esmond went out, vastly relieved that Belinda wasn't coming with him. He strode up the meadow towards the wall and the pine wood and once he was out of sight of the Hall hurried along to Jeremy's cabin.

His friend and accomplice (as he now thought of him) was sitting on the steps enjoying a cup of tea. He was unusually well dressed in a tweed suit.

'I'm afraid the wedding isn't until nine o'clock tonight,' Esmond said. 'That clergyman has six other weddings today. Sorry about that.'

'Nothing to worry about. Anyway, I've finished cleaning the chapel and even polished that tombstone,' he said. 'It's got the strangest inscription on it. You'll never guess what it says.'

'The name of that skeleton bloke underneath?'

Jeremy shook his head. 'Not on your life. No one's name. Want to try again?'

Esmond shook his head. 'No idea. What does it say?'

'You really want to know?'

'Of course. Don't keep me in suspense.'

'All right. It says, "Who takes me from my tomb will meet his doom. Who does not let me lie in peace will never die in peace. Hell awaits the stranger's hand. Best be off my precious land." Grisly threats, don't you think?'

'Certainly very weird. Why didn't we see this yesterday when we used the jack to lift that slab?' asked Esmond.

'Because it hadn't been cleaned for goodness only knows how many centuries. It was only when I used metal polish time after time that I spotted it.'

'Very peculiar,' said Esmond, dismissing it from his mind.

That evening Esmond was back in the Hall dressed in his suit and his brand-new shoes. To his surprise, Belinda introduced her bridesmaid, an ancient old woman who he could only suppose was some kind of Grope retainer or nanny. Myrtle had sent word from her room that she was much too poorly to attend and no one else from the family had been invited to join them.

They sat in the big drawing room and chatted while waiting for the Rev. Horston who arrived looking, as Belinda had predicted, tired but on time at nine o'clock. He was clearly relieved that there were no guests.

'Ah well, we may as well proceed with the ceremony,' he said as they rose and, led by the bridegroom, crossed the courtyard to the tiny chapel where Old Samuel had lit an inordinate number of candles. Outside the sun was setting but the chapel windows were so small and splendidly stained that even the weary parson was impressed. Esmond introduced Old Samuel as his best man and the Rev. Horston conducted the marriage remarkably quickly and without any awkward questions. Belinda had been right: he wanted to get back to his vicarage and go to bed as soon as he could. She gave him several hundred pounds more than he had expected and he drove off a well-contented man.

Once he'd left Old Samuel opened a bottle of excellent champagne and toasted the happy couple and an hour later Mr and Mrs Grope went to a large bed in a bedroom at the far end of the house where they thought that their lovemaking couldn't be overheard. Finally exhausted they went to sleep.

It was another week before Esmond gathered together his courage and decided that although his lady wife seemed to be behaving herself he really must put his scheme into practice. He was in the middle of rehearsing his conversation with Belinda with only the piglets to bear witness to his extreme nervousness when Jeremy found him and asked him if he would come up to his cabin.

'I haven't yet given you a wedding present,' he said when Esmond arrived.

'But there's no need to do that, really there isn't.'

'Oh but there is, Joe. You've been the first person to be a true friend to me ever since I arrived at Grope Hall and started being Old Samuel instead of Young Jeremy.' He looked sad for a moment before brightening. 'See that sack with tar all over it in the corner. That's my present to you. Go on, open it.'

Esmond still hesitated. 'I'm serious. You don't have to give me anything. I've got everything I want. Well, I will have if everything goes to plan.'

'I insist, Joe. You're my best friend. We shook hands on that, remember.'

'I do indeed and I'll always be your friend.'

'Look at your present for me then.'

'Well, if you insist.'

Esmond crossed the room and after some difficulty

managed to unwind the copper wire which held the sack closed. As he did so it fell over and some coins spilt out and lay scattered on the floor. Esmond stared at them in amazement. He had never seen money like this before. He picked one up and examined it. It was a gold sovereign. There was no doubt in his mind and as if to confirm his belief the sack itself was terribly heavy.

'There must be a fortune here. Where on earth did you find it?' he gasped.

'There is. I reckon several million. As for where I found it, can't you guess?'

Esmond tried to guess. Finally he shook his head. 'You're not going to tell me under that great slab you were polishing?' he said, slumping into a chair.

'Spot on.'

Esmond gaped at him. 'But it was so heavy. You can't have lifted it yourself.'

'I rigged up a sort of crane from a tractor and fastened a whacking great chain to one end of the slab and winched it up that way while you were having it off with Mrs Grope after the wedding.'

'But someone must have heard you,' said Esmond.

'With the racket you and your missus were making? You're joking! Anyway, the chapel's some way from the Hall. After I'd done that it was simple. I just moved our skeleton friend to one side and kept shoving in a metal rod until I felt something. Then I dug down and somehow hauled this sack up. It took me all night and God knows I was shattered. I slept all day and most of the next night.'

'I'm not surprised. How did you get the sack up here? It weighs a ton.'

'The tractor again. The tractor with a wheelbarrow tied behind it.'

Esmond stared at him silently in still more amazement mingled with admiration.

Jeremy broke the silence.

'Well, you're a very rich man now. You can do what you like, buy what you like, go where you like. You can – '

'Balls!' Esmond exploded. 'I know what I'm going to do, or rather we are. We're going to go halves. You found the stuff which is more than I could ever have done in a million years though how the hell you knew it was there I can't even begin to imagine.'

Jeremy laughed. 'Think of that iron slab and the inscription on it in lousy verse. That told me there was something more than a skeleton with a spade down there, though I didn't expect it would be a fortune in gold sovereigns.'

'Which we're splitting because of our genuine friendship. And now I'd better be getting back to the Hall. I've something to say to my new bride.'

Esmond found Belinda in the garden with a large bunch of red roses which she was putting in a bowl.

'Isn't it wonderful to be here,' she said. 'I loved it as a child when I visited in the summer but it's even better now I've escaped from that dreadful Albert and his horrible bungalow. You've no idea how I hated living there.'

'I can imagine,' said Esmond who, now that he thought about it, really could imagine how dreadful life with his uncle must have been. Even more alarmingly, the very thought of Belinda in another man's arms made him feel quite ill. Whatever had come over him?

'You're never going back there, Belinda,' he began, adopting a stern look. 'You're going to stay here and you're going to damned well do as I say from now on. I've been thinking about it and I love the peaceful natural life I have here and I'm going to stay and be a farmer but I can't hold with you slipping me sleeping tablets and telling me what to do and say all the time. I want a proper wife: one who looks after me properly else there's going to be hell to pay. And what's more Old Samuel isn't going to be called Old Samuel any longer. It isn't even his name. He's going to be called Jeremy, Young Jeremy for now and then when he's old, Old Jeremy. And what's even more, Old Samuel – I mean Young Jeremy – isn't going to work for us any more because he and I are going to go into partnership. He's come into some money and we've decided that we're going to go into business breeding bulls as well as running the farm. You're to have nothing to do with any of it although you can feed the piglets from time to time if you've a mind to . . . And, and . . .'

246

'Well, you're the boss, my love. You make the decisions.'

Esmond looked at Belinda in astonishment.

'But you said only the other day that we had to stick to the old traditions and now – '

'What's the point of trying to follow an ancient and clearly barbaric tradition? We are equals. It's as simple as that. If we have a baby girl she can follow the tradition of the past if she so wishes but for my part I rather hope that we have a boy.'

And on that note she carried the bowl of roses into the house.

The Wilt Inheritance

Read on for an extract of Tom Sharpe's new novel . . .

Chapter 1

Wilt drove down to Fenland University feeling in a thoroughly bad mood. He'd had a row with his wife, Eva, the previous night about the expense of sending their four daughters to boarding school when, to Wilt's opinion, they had been doing very well at their old school, the Convent. Eva, however, had been adamant that the quads must stay at the private school.

'They've got to learn good manners and they weren't doing that at the Convent. And in any case, you swear so often they've become quite foul-mouthed and I'm not having it. They're better off away from home.'

'If you had to fill in totally useless forms and supposedly teach Computer Studies to the illiterates I'm lumbered with – who actually know far more about using the bally gadgets than I do – you would swear too,' Wilt had said, choosing not to point out that since they'd become teenagers the quads' repertoire of obscenities put his own to shame.

'I can't afford to carry on paying for another God knows how many years just so that you can boast to the damn neighbours about where your damn daughters go to school. The Convent was already costing a small fortune, as you well know.'

Altogether it had been a most acrimonious evening. To make matters worse, Wilt had not been exaggerating. His salary really was so small he couldn't see how he was going to go on paying the boarding-school fees and still maintain the modest standard of living the family presently enjoyed. As merely Head of the so-called Communications Department he was paid less than the heads of academic departments, all re-titled Professors when Fenland College of Arts and Technology had been designated a University and, as a result, earning a great deal more than him. Eva had, of course, made that point several times over during their row.

'If you'd had the gumption to leave years ago, like Patrick Mottram, you could have got a really decent job with a much better salary in a proper university. But, oh, no, you had to stay on at that stupid technical college because "I've got too many good friends there". Utter rubbish! You've No Get Up And Go in you, that's what you've got.'

At that Wilt got up and went. By the time he got back from the pub, resolving to have it out with Eva once and for all, she had given up on him and gone to bed.

But as he drove into the 'University' car park the next day, Wilt had to admit to himself that she was right. He ought to have left years ago. He hated the wretched Communications Department and actually could probably number his friends still working there on one finger. He should probably have left Eva too. Come to think of it, he should never have married such an infernally bossy woman in the first place. She never did things by halves: the quads were proof of that.

Wilt's spirits sank even lower when he thought of his daughters, all four of them exact replicas of his ghastly wife and just as loud and overbearing as she was. No, *more* loud and overbearing than she was given the combined effect of their quadruple efforts. All four girls were inexhaustible in their petty squabbling and inter-sororial battles, and he was pretty sure that the demise of his get up and go had pretty much coincided with their arrival.

There had been a moment in their early infancy when, in between the nappies and bottles and the disgusting pap-like baby food Eva insisted on shovelling into them, he had briefly entertained great hopes for his offspring, imagining shining futures ahead of them. But the older they grew the worse their behaviour became, from torturing the cat to tormenting the neighbours – though pinning anything on any one of them was impossible since they all looked exactly the same. He supposed that at least now they were boarders they were someone else's problem, although it was a bloody steep price to pay for it.

Wilt cheered up on his arrival when he found a note inside a sealed envelope on his desk. It was from the Chief Administrator, Mr Vark, telling him that his presence was not required at the meeting of the recently created Academic Apportionment Committee. Wilt thanked God he didn't have to attend. He wasn't sure he had the patience to sit through another interminable session of paper-shuffling and self-important pronouncements about nothing.

Feeling in a better mood, he went off to check the classrooms but found them largely empty except for a few stray students who were playing on the computers. It was the end of the summer term in a week's time and with no exams in the offing most of the staff and students saw no point in sticking around. Not that the lazy sods stuck around much in the first place. Wilt was back at his desk, making yet another attempt to sort out the following term's timetable, when Peter Braintree, the Professor of English, poked his face round the door.

'Are you coming to Vark's latest nonsensical gathering, Henry?' he asked.

'No, I'm bloody well not. Vark has sent me a note

saying I'm to stay away and for once I'm going to do what he wants.'

'I don't blame you. Rotten waste of time. Wish I could get out of it as well, I've got stacks of exam papers to mark.' Braintree paused. 'I suppose you wouldn't think of . . .'

'No, I wouldn't,' Wilt said firmly. 'Mark your own papers. Can't you see I'm occupied?' He waved airily at the timetable in front of him. 'I'm working out how to fit the Digital Future into Thursday afternoon.'

Braintree had long since given up trying to make sense of any of Wilt's more obscure remarks. He simply shrugged his shoulders and let the door bang loudly behind him.

Wilt gave up the timetable as a bad job, and for the rest of the morning sat filling in the forms the Administration Department concocted practically every day to justify employing more staff than the 'University' had lecturers.

'Suppose it keeps the sods off the street,' he muttered to himself, 'just like having so many so-called students makes the employment figures look far better than they really are.' He could feel his bad temper returning.

After lunch he sat for an hour in the Staff Room, reading the newspapers piled up there. As usual they were filled with horror stories. A pregnant woman had been stabbed in the back for no apparent reason

255

by a twelve year old boy; four louts had kicked an old man to death in his own garage; and fifteen insane murderers had been released from Broadmoor after five years – presumably because they hadn't been allowed to kill anyone in that time. And that was in the *Daily Times*. Wilt tried the *Graphic* and found it just as sickening. In the end he skipped the political pages, which were full of lies, and decided to go for some air. He went out to the park and was walking round it when he spotted a familiar figure sitting on a bench.

To his surprise Wilt realised it was his old adversary Inspector Flint. He crossed over and sat down beside him.

'What on earth are you doing here?' he asked.

'As a matter of fact, I was sitting here wondering what you were getting up to.'

'Not a very interesting topic. I should have thought you'd have been concentrating on something more in your line,' said Wilt.

'Like what?'

'Oh, arresting innocent people perhaps. You're good at that. Trying to convince yourself that they're criminals. I know you were certain I was one when I was idiotic enough to dump that beastly inflatable doll down a pile hole, but I was drunk at the time and anyway it was years ago.'

Flint nodded. 'Quite. Then there was the drug stunt and the terrorist business in Willington Road. You were involved in all those rotten affairs. Not intentionally, I agree, but it's interesting how you repeatedly seem to find yourself in the middle of particularly curious situations. There must be something criminal about you for you to get caught up in quite so many criminal activities, don't you think?'

'No I don't think. And nor, quite often, do you. Though you've got a really fantastic imagination, I'll grant you that, Inspector.'

'Not me, Henry. Oh, definitely not me. I'm just quoting your old friend, and my old colleague, Mr Hodge. Superintendent Hodge to you, of course Wilt. And I can tell you, Mr Hodge still hasn't forgotten the quagmire you led him into over that drug business . . . nor has he ever got over it. Speaking frankly, I myself don't think you could commit a real crime if it was handed you on a plate. You're a talker, not a doer.'

Wilt sighed. The Inspector was only too damned right. But did everyone have to keep reminding him of how impotent he was?

'Well, apart from thinking about me, what on earth are you doing sitting out here?' he asked. 'Have you retired or something?'

'Been thinking seriously about that too,' said Flint. 'I think I may do. I'm never given anything interesting to do, thanks to that bastard Hodge. He goes and marries the Chief Constable's daughter, and gets promoted to Superintendent as a result, while I'm desk-bound, filling in forms and doing nothing but paperwork. It's as boring as hell.'

'Join the club,' said Wilt in spite of himself. He hated the expression. 'I'm doing the same. Forms, agendas, bumf of all sorts . . . and all I get in return is hell from Eva when I go home because I earn a miserable salary and she insists on our paying a small fortune to send the quads to an expensive boarding school. God alone knows how we're going to continue doing it.'

They chatted on, grumbling about the economy and politicians in general, and it was some considerable time before Wilt glanced at his watch and realised it was later than he'd thought. He wondered if the Academic Apportionment Committee meeting had ended yet.

He said goodbye to Flint and went back to his office. It was past four o'clock before Braintree stuck his head round the door again, this time with the news that he'd only nipped out for a pee and the committee was still at it hammer and tongs.

'You were bloody sensible deciding not to go even if Vark would have let you. They're all having a hell of a row. Mostly the usual topics,' he said. 'Anyway I'll definitely be finished by six. Do you want to hang on for me?'

'Suppose so – I've nothing better to do with myself. Thank God I kept away,' Wilt muttered as Braintree hurried back out. For the remainder of the afternoon

Wilt sat in the Staff Room, occasionally wondering about Inspector Flint's assessment of his ability to attract crime. 'I am a talker, not a doer,' he said to himself. He'd have given anything to have had the old Fenland Tech back. He'd had a sense of doing something useful in those years, even if that only amounted to having arguments with apprentice technicians and making them think.

By the time Braintree returned Wilt was thoroughly depressed.

'You look as if you've seen a ghost,' Braintree said.

'I have. The ghost of things past and opportunities lost. As for the future . . .'

'What you need is a stiff drink, old chap.'

'You're damned right I do and it won't be a pint of beer this time. Whisky is what I need.'

'So do I after that verbal punch up.'

'Was the meeting as bad as all that?'

'Let's just say that in the end it couldn't have been much worse . . . Which pub do you want to go to?'

'In my present mood I suggest the Hangman's Arms. It will be quiet and I'll be able to walk, or at least stumble, home from there,' said Wilt.

'I'll say! By the time I've had a few, I'm not going to risk driving either. Nowadays those buggers will breathalyse you as soon as look at you if you're within a bloody mile of a pub.'

There was no one in the bar when they entered.

The place was as grim as its name, and the barman looked as though he'd been a hangman himself once and, given the opportunity, would be happy to demonstrate his skills on either of them.

'Well, what's it to be?' he asked gruffly.

'Two double Scotches and go easy with the soda,' Braintree told him.

Wilt noted the order and sat down in a dark and grubby corner. The situation must be genuinely dire for Peter Braintree to order doubles and go easy on the soda.

'Well,' Wilt grunted when his friend brought the drinks over to the round table, 'spit it out. Was it that bad? Yes, clearly it was. Out with it then.'

'I'd say "Cheers" but in the circumstances . . . Well, mud in your eye!'

'All I want to know is, have I been given the boot?'

Braintree shook his head and sighed.

'No, but you're not out of the woods yet,' he said. 'You were saved by the Vice-Chancellor. Correction: the Vice-Principal. Sorry, I know how you feel about these pompous new titles. As you're bound to know also, Mayfield was in the Chair and doesn't exactly like you.'

Wilt bridled.

'That's the understatement of the decade.'

'Agreed. But he loathes Dr Board even more, and since Board is Head of Modern languages, and languages are vital if they're going to go on calling the place a university, there's damn all Mayfield can do to get rid of him. So, because you're a friend of Board, and because Mayfield doesn't like you in the first place, it was starting to look bad for Computer Studies . . .'

'Meaning my job *is* at stake?'

'Well, yes, but wait for it: the Vice-Principal came to your rescue by pointing out that the Communications Faculty . . . sorry, the Communications Department . . . has many more students than any other, and now that History has gone and Maths is down to around forty which is even lower than Science, the Univers— the College can't afford to dispense with Communications. And that includes you.'

'Why? They could find someone else to take my place.'

'The V-P doesn't think so. He put the boot into Mayfield by asking him if he'd care to volunteer to take your job on, and Mayfield said he wouldn't dream of dealing with the hooligans in your department. Oh, yes, the V-P had him by the short and curlies there! Mayfield had gone quite white by then but the Vice-Principal still hadn't finished. He said you handled the brutes very deftly and . . .'

'That's very decent of him. Did he actually say "deftly"?'

'His exact word, and he was backed up by Board who said you had a real gift plus years of experience in dealing with blighters *he* wouldn't go near with an

AK47 or something even more lethal. At one point he called you "something of a genius".'

Wilt gulped at his whisky.

'I must say, Board's always been a good friend,' he murmured. 'But he's gone above and beyond this time. No wonder Vark didn't want me there.' He looked down at his glass gloomily. 'They may be hooligans but some of my lads are good-hearted enough. The main thing is to let them get on with what they really like to do.'

'You mean, muck around playing games and surfing the internet for porn?'

Wilt shook his head.

'They can't get on to the pornography sites. I got a couple of technicians over from Electronics to block that area off, and in any case it costs money to download the really hard filth and none of my lot have credit cards. Or only ones they've stolen from someone, of course, which don't usually work on the internet.'

'Oh, well, that puts paid to Mayfield's argument that they should never have forced all those computers on to you,' Braintree said.

Wilt finished his whisky.

'Shouldn't have closed the old Tech down,' he declared. 'Still, I've got something to celebrate. At least my job's safe for the time being and the Vice-Principal isn't going to resign any time soon. He earns such a whacking great salary, lucky bugger, and so long as he's around it sounds as though dear Professor

Mayfield's scuppered. I'm going to have another Scotch. No, don't move. I'll get them.'

This time he ordered triples.

'I'd love to have seen Mayfield go white. He's no more a professor than I am. Let's drink to the V-P . . . and to Dr Board.'

ALSO AVAILABLE IN ARROW

Wilt

Tom Sharpe

'This delightful book . . . lives, rises and triumphs by a slicing wit'
Daily Mirror

'Superb farce . . . If you don't laugh your head off, Crippen wasn't
guilty'
Tribune

'Mr Sharpe's face has a gritty satirical edge to it, and the world his
embattled central character inhabits is all too real'
Sunday Times

'Tom Sharpe piles slapstick upon slapstick with the ingenious
dexterity of a music-hall illusionist'
Sunday Telegraph

'The funniest detective story in years'
Evening News

arrow books

ALSO AVAILABLE IN ARROW

Porterhouse Blue

Tom Sharpe

'That rarest and most joyous of products – a highly intelligent and
funny book'
Sunday Times

'Terrific. It is light years since I read anything so original . . . (the)
character drawing is wonderful . . a very good book'
P.G. Wodehouse

'A toppling house of comic cards that knock you flat. He is the
funniest writer to have emerged for years'
Observer

'This supremely entertaining book is guaranteed to make you laugh'
Books and Bookmen

'Tom Sharpe makes me laugh loud and long . . . he offers so much
to delight in'
Ion Trewain, *The Times*

arrow books